Counselor

Theirs was
 no ordinary
 friendship . . .

　　　　　　. . . but then, he was
　　　　　　　　no ordinary
　　　　　　　　　　friend.

ANN ASCHAUER

© 2003 by Ann Aschauer. All rights reserved

Printed in the United States of America

Packaged by Pleasant Word, a division of WinePress Publishing, PO Box 428, Enumclaw, WA 98022. The views expressed or implied in this work do not necessarily reflect those of Pleasant Word, a division of WinePress Publishing. The author(s) is ultimately responsible for the design, content and editorial accuracy of this work.

No part of this publication may be reproduced, stored in a retrieval system or transmitted in any way by any means—electronic, mechanical, photocopy, recording or otherwise—without the prior permission of the copyright holder, except as provided by USA copyright law.

Unless otherwise noted, all Scriptures are taken from the Holy Bible, New International Version, Copyright © 1973, 1978, 1984 by the International Bible Society. Used by permission of Zondervan Publishing House. The "NIV" and "New International Version" trademarks are registered in the United States Patent and Trademark Office by International Bible Society.

Scripture references marked KJV are taken from the King James Version of the Bible.

Scripture references marked NASB are taken from the New American Standard Bible, © 1960, 1963, 1968, 1971, 1972, 1973, 1975, 1977 by The Lockman Foundation. Used by permission.

ISBN 1-57921-527-0
Library of Congress Catalog Card Number: 2002115820

Dedication

To Marty, Joanna, Ben, and Kelly—I love you very much!

Sean and Rachel, you are answers to a mother's prayers. Welcome to the family!

Dad, Susie, Kelly and family, Dave, Larry, Eunyi, Harry and Sandy, Glen and Arliene, Julie, Aaron, Robin, Lucy, Carol, Peggy, Carly, Matt, and Ed, thanks for all your feedback, encouragement, help, and support.

To my students at Landmark, for helping me see through young eyes.

And of course, to J, thanks for the inspiration.

Prologue

How had she managed to get herself into this mess?

Liz stood on the stage, her heart pounding as the house lights dimmed and the curtain rose. Somewhat dazed, she gazed out into the audience, where the sea of faces blurred together into one threatening entity.

Her hands hung at her sides, caressed by the folds of her velvet gown. Her hair was held back with tortoiseshell combs, a pair of ringlets dangling flirtatiously at her neck. Her makeup was set, and her rhinestone earrings glistened in the spotlight where she stood poised and waiting; all systems were "go."

In the wings, unseen by the audience, a shadowy figure gripped his headset, looked up at the actors, and signaled to them to start.

But as Liz listened to the other actor speaking the vaguely familiar opening lines of the play, panic set in; she was drawing a blank.

She knew her line was next, but what it was she had no idea. She tried hard to visualize the script, scene one. Now the lines weren't even familiar. The other actor finished speaking and there was dead silence. Time for Liz's line. By now all she could hear was the thundering of her own heart, which seemed to grow and fill the entire theater. And *she was finding to her horror that now she couldn't remember a thing—not a line, what part she was playing, not even the name of the play.*

As the alarm split the morning with an obnoxious buzz, Liz awoke with a gasp and fumbled for the clock in the dim light. Her groping fingers finally found the "off" button, and with a sigh she flopped back, her auburn curls scattering as her head sank deep into the pillow.

"*Man*, I *hate* that dream!" she grumbled to herself.

It might have been the recent stress of auditions that had brought it back. Somehow the sight of a director and stage manager sitting with pads, pens, and blank expressions on their faces was more terrifying to her than a whole auditorium full of relatives, friends, and innocent strangers. It even could have been the fear that she might actually have landed a part this time. As much as Liz dreaded failure, success could be frightening as well, because it meant now people were expecting something from her.

But most likely this recurring nightmare was the timid girl's expression of her dread of life itself, which (admit it) is one big improvisation. She much preferred the security of a script. Having been raised in a home where etiquette was modeled and taught so one would know the rules and be prepared to do and say the "right" thing in any and every social situation, Liz had found the real world bewildering, as most people she encountered seemed to be living by their own set of rules—or no rules at all.

You might think it odd for a young girl as timid as Liz to seek a career as an actress. But to those who understand the theater, it makes perfect sense; if you don't want to deal with the world, with reality—with life itself—the stage is the perfect place to hide.

But, as Liz was about to find out, you can't hide forever.

Chapter One

The University of Illinois's Urbana campus sat in the middle of the state like a beehive in a cornfield. In contrast to its surroundings—one farm after another, wide-open spaces serenaded by a plethora of country music stations—the U of I Campus teemed with humanity, culture, research, noise, and stimulating activity of every kind.

The university was a study in contrasts. At a major crossroads one could see a large bronze statue of "Alma Mater," green with age, arms eternally outstretched ("TO THY HAPPY CHILDREN OF THE FUTURE, THOSE OF THE PAST SEND GREETINGS") as an imposing bright blue bus roared by with the words "ILLINOIS: Fighting Illini" in massive orange letters.

Likewise, the more than 36,000 students came in all sizes, colors, and majors, each with a head full of goals and a heart full of dreams. They frequently left run-down dwellings that appeared to be held together with paint to attend class in impressive, newly built complexes or classic structures that looked as if they had been there forever.

As for Krannert Center for the Performing Arts, from the outside it resembled a collection of drive-in movie theaters. Several immense, abstract extensions of the complex reached skyward, towering over visitors like the mountains of an alien planet.

Inside, although Krannert had a spacious lobby with parquet floors and marble walls to impress the public, the areas most used by the students were windowless rooms and corridors of gray cement-block walls, gray concrete floors, and fluorescent lights; even the greenroom wasn't green.

Outside the department offices the tension that morning was thick as greasepaint as students loitered around the bulletin board. It was apparent that hardly anyone had had much sleep, but these troopers had roused themselves to be present for the big event: the posting of the cast for the spring musical. For the most part it was superficial chatter. One student in particular tried hard to seem as nonchalant and lighthearted as the others, tossing her auburn curls with a laugh to hide her growing sense of desperation.

Liz Danfield was a slender, attractive would-be actress with large, bashful green eyes and a distinction she hoped no one else had picked up on. Although this was the last semester of her senior year, she had yet to land a major role. It seemed as though every other acting major had played at least one lead role in the various productions put on by the university. Some had even appeared in local TV commercials. But for Liz, play tryouts had repeatedly been a bitter disappointment. Liz had had ample opportunities to work with costumes, scenery, props, lighting, and makeup; she figured she should get the prize for more backstage experience than any other acting major. She was far better acquainted with the "techies" than with the other actors.

Oh well, she thought, *maybe this show will be different.* After all, she practically knew *The Sound of Music* by heart, and she was a natural for the eldest daughter. Other roles she had tried for might have made her extremely uncomfortable anyway. Once she had actually fled the audition upon finding out that, were she to get the part, she would be expected to shed her clothes. Thus she had earned herself the reputation of being "inhibited"—not a very useful label to wear in the world of theater.

Chapter One

But for once the musical had a clean story line and decent songs, and on the day of tryouts Liz had not been battling the usual laryngitis; she actually felt she had sung well. Her hopes were high, but mixed with them was the ominous threat of despair that loomed so close. *If I don't land this role*, a part of her fretted, *I may as well quit.* Her knees felt weak, but outwardly, like the alien cliffs of Krannert, she wore the facade of one who would never be shaken one way or another.

At the click of the opening door every head turned in expectation, and the cluster of students parted just enough to allow the stage manager to reach the bulletin board and post the much-anticipated sheet of paper. The poor woman could barely work her way back through the crowd that immediately closed in like the waters of the Red Sea to inspect the list.

Liz hung back. She was familiar with this ritual. Shrieks and squeals and hugs followed as congratulations were shared. Her speech partner, Amber, flushed with pleasure, squeezed out through the crowd, breathing an excited "Yesss!" Her eyes met Liz's.

"I got it!" she squealed.

"Congratulations," Liz replied, trying to be happy for her.

"Thanks," said Amber, beaming.

"Uh, when you were up there, did you happen to see . . . my name?"

"Sorry," Amber shrugged. "I didn't see the whole list." A giggle escaped her; she sounded downright giddy. "Once I saw my name, I kinda lost track of everything else!" She grinned at several students who were shouting their congratulations.

The knot in Liz's stomach was growing tighter as she realized no one was congratulating her. She stepped aside, hoping not to be noticed as the students left in clusters for their morning classes. Most of them trailed past her as though she were invisible, but one student with freckles, sandy hair, and a friendly smile called out to her as he passed.

"Hey, Liz! Congratulations!" Liz gave him a puzzled look. "Didn't you see the list yet? You were chosen! Way to go!"

"Huh? Thanks, Sean," Liz stammered as hope began to rise again.

The young man gave her a thumbs up and a wink and was gone.

As the excited chatter of the students echoed through the halls, Liz stepped up to the bulletin board with some apprehension.

Amber's name was at the top of the column marked "Cast." As expected, Liz didn't see her name on that list. Once again the part she had coveted had been given to Colleen Thompson, an acting major who had had a major role every semester that Liz could remember. Liz checked the list of understudies; nope. Finally she glanced down a long list of chorus members, mostly freshmen, and there was her name at the bottom of the list. The first twenty names were listed in alphabetical order, so it was apparent that Liz had been an afterthought. She bit her lip and turned to go.

She was surprised to see Amber coming out of the ladies' room, slipping a compact back into her purse. A fresh coat of red lipstick glistened as she grinned at Liz, still reveling in her triumph. Liz bravely forced a smile.

"Hey, Danfield! Wanna go get some coffee?" Amber asked. Liz was not exactly Amber's dearest friend, but all of Amber's buddies had class first hour, and since this was unusually early for her, she must have figured coffee with Liz was better than hanging out alone until her first class. Besides, she obviously wanted an excuse to talk about the show.

"Sure, I guess we have time before second hour." Liz hoped Amber hadn't heard the catch in her voice and wondered if the burning sensation in her eyes meant they were turning red.

The two young women arrived at the Commons Cafeteria in the Student Union just in time to get a table before the morning rush. The moment they sat down a noisy flood of students poured through the door, and every table was taken.

"Whoa, made it just in time!" Amber exclaimed. Liz said nothing but sat staring at her cup with a faraway look. Amber was beginning to wonder if coffee alone would have been such a bad idea after all. Both girls knew Amber was elated; both knew Liz was dejected and not in any mood to fawn over her successful class-

Chapter One

mate. The unsatisfying situation left them both looking for a totally new subject of conversation.

At the moment the most interesting thing in the room was the plight of a handicapped student. He was a gaunt young man with a beard and dark hair pulled back in an elastic band. Wearing thick glasses and dangling a white cane over one arm, he walked with a heavy limp and held his tray with shaking hands.

"Do you know him?" Liz asked.

Amber turned around. "No. I've seen him around, but I don't know who he is. Or what his problem is." She stiffened and looked away.

"Poor guy, there are no free tables, and he's about to drop that tray." Liz looked at the empty chair at their table. "Do you mind...?"

"No, go ahead," Amber replied, although her tone of voice clearly registered disgust. Liz ignored it.

Stepping over to the student, she touched his arm. "There's a free seat at our table. You're welcome to join us, if you'd like."

The young man squinted in the direction of their table, where Amber stared ahead uncomfortably.

"Thank you so much," the young man said in a voice that was barely intelligible. With difficulty, he made his way to the table and set down the tray, now complete with spilled coffee and soggy napkins; it seemed a relief for him to sit down. Amber took a deep breath and glanced around to see if anyone she knew happened to be in the vicinity.

"Thank you," the student said to Amber, ignoring the fact that she had had nothing to do with the invitation. "My name is J—." Even if it had been clearly stated, the rest of the name would have been lost in the growing din of the crowd.

Amber replied, "Hi," unenthusiastically.

"I'm Liz and this is Amber," Liz bubbled with forced animation to make up for Amber's rudeness. "What did you say your name was again?"

"It's J—." Again the noise of the cafeteria drowned out the name. Liz feared that to ask a third time might call attention to his speech impediment, so she just said, "Nice to meet you."

Just then a pair of teachers from the theater department entered the room, gesturing dramatically as they conversed. Amber stood up abruptly.

"Excuse me," she said. "I've got to get to class." Class was not for another forty minutes, but Amber's eyes told Liz, *Don't say it, I know. Just let me get out of here!*

Liz understood. Amber could be nice, usually when she wanted something, but she was not one to be seen with the "wrong kind of people." She liked to be with the cool crowd, and Liz was about as "un-cool" as Amber condescended to; this guy, with his spilled coffee and clumsy speech, was definitely not in her league. Liz often thought that if she had not been assigned to be her partner in speech class, Amber would have had nothing to do with her, either.

"She's not like you, is she?" the young man asked after an awkward pause, his mouth forming the words with some difficulty.

It took a moment for what he had said to sink in, partly because of his handicap, and because Liz was caught off guard by the question. Her first thought was, *Yeah, she's a winner, I'm a loser*, but what she said was, "What do you mean, *like me*?"

He smiled warmly and said simply, "Kind."

Liz sighed, already tired of pretending to be cheerful. "Kindness doesn't get you far in this world," she muttered.

"Oh, you'd be surprised," he said cryptically. Liz paused for a moment to puzzle over what he could have meant, then attempted to explain away Amber's insensitivity.

"Amber just got a big part in a play. She's probably going to tell all her friends. I guess that's understandable." She sighed.

The young man seemed uninterested in Amber. "So," he began, "tell me about Liz."

Again she was caught off guard, first by his straightforwardness, then by the relative ease with which she was able to understand him now. "What about me?" she asked cautiously.

"Well, for starters," he began quietly, "why do you feel like a loser?"

Chapter One

Liz was startled to find someone she had just met to be so intuitive and at the same time so blunt. She started to deny or protest, but somehow she knew she couldn't deceive this person. Although he was virtually blind, she had the feeling that through those thick lenses, he was looking straight into her soul. At first the feeling made her uneasy, but as she saw the sympathetic look in his eyes, she decided he might be a safe person to "dump" on. After all, who in her world would be interested in even communicating with such a person, much less hearing her deepest, darkest secrets from him? Who would even suspect that he knew?

"I . . . I don't know where to begin."

"How about the beginning?" he smiled. "I've got lots of time."

"Well," she began, looking into her steaming cup, as though she might find in it some way to start explaining herself. "I decided before I even came here as a freshman that I wanted to be a theater major."

Liz went on to confess that she had come to the U of I theater department mainly to be with a certain person, who had turned out to be not at all the person she had thought he was. And as she told this stranger about her theatrical career—or lack thereof— she felt such acceptance that it was a relief to be able to speak openly without having to feign indifference. She found herself telling him about all her disappointments and frustrations. She spoke at first in general terms, but by the time she and the gentle stranger were on their second round of coffee, she found herself relating more detailed accounts of specific wounds; she was surprised at how many existed.

As she spoke, the young man looked intently at her, his face showing the utmost compassion. Somehow she knew that in spite of the noise surrounding them, he was hearing every word. And she could tell he understood. So she continued to unload, sensing no judgment or condemnation.

Nearly half an hour later, it occurred to her who it was to whom she had been complaining so freely; suddenly she felt ashamed. She stopped abruptly and stammered, "Oh, listen to me, whining and complaining about my measly problems! You probably know a lot more about suffering than I do!" She immediately wondered if perhaps she should not have said such a thing, and she studied his face to see if she had offended him. Instead, she saw the same understanding in his eyes.

"Oh, suffering comes in many forms," he said quietly. "Rejection is definitely one of them." The image of Amber's abrupt departure flashed across Liz's mind.

"I guess you've seen your share of that, too." Again she second guessed herself as to whether that had been an appropriate comment, but he just smiled thoughtfully.

"I'm familiar with it," he said softly, and Liz noticed that she could now understand his words as easily as she could anyone else's. *Perhaps*, she thought, *it's because we're not that different after all?*

Liz wondered what his physical problems might be, but had begun to doubt the wisdom of thinking out loud as she had been doing for the past thirty minutes. So there was a brief silence, after which her friend finally spoke.

"Cerebral palsy."

"What?"

"I have cerebral palsy. Isn't that what you were wondering?"

"Oh, I wasn't won—I mean, I wasn't going to ask . . ."

"But you were wondering. It's OK, it's perfectly natural to wonder." His smile once again put her at ease. "And I'm legally blind. I see light and colors and vague shapes, but I can't read or drive. I was born with both the CP and the blindness. In a way, I'm fortunate I've always had them; it's saved me the trouble of adjusting."

Liz felt so safe with him by now that she asked directly, "Will it get any worse?"

"Not really," he replied. "I'm lucky in that, too. As for rejection, I've always experienced it, and so I've never expected anything else. You, on the other hand, have had high hopes." Liz nodded and looked down; it was true. "Expectations can make all the difference," he continued. "For example, I would guess that you are very pretty."

Chapter One

"You can tell that?" Liz asked, then became embarrassed that she had confirmed his guess and might have come across as being immodest.

"I heard a young man at the next table comment to his friend," he explained. "He may have thought I was deaf as well as blind. I'm sure he was wondering what a beautiful young thing such as you is doing with an ugly duckling like me." There was no trace of self-pity in his voice, and he winked at Liz. She smiled back, then looked down at her cup awkwardly, thinking she should say something, but not knowing what. But the young man didn't seem to be expecting any comment. He continued.

"You've been under the impression that your beauty entitles you to live happily ever after, haven't you?" He paused to sip his coffee and to let the statement sink in.

Liz thought about it for a moment. Did she really think that? She blushed, ashamed at the thought and a little annoyed with him for pointing out the possibility of such arrogance.

"It's not your fault," he added kindly. "You've no doubt been taught to think that way from the day you were old enough to hear a fairy tale. They all end the same way: the good people—the beautiful ones—live happily ever after. The ugly people are the bad ones. But that isn't the real world."

It certainly isn't, Liz thought, remembering the shallowness of her pretty friend, and looking at this one whom she earlier might have considered merely an odd specimen of humanity. Now she was seeing him with growing appreciation.

"And no point in looking for 'happily ever after.' It doesn't exist, except in fairy tales. But," he added, "that's just as well. 'Happily ever after' isn't all it's cracked up to be."

"What do you mean?" Liz asked, intrigued by the unexpected statement, and by the certainty in his voice.

"Think about it," he said. "When you hear 'and they lived happily ever after,' what happens next?"

"Nothing," she said. "That's the end of the story." She wasn't sure what he was getting at.

The young man pointed a crooked finger at her. "*Exactly!*" he declared.

"'They lived happily ever after' is just another way of saying, 'Nothing interesting or exciting happened to them after that.'"

Liz thought for a moment and found herself smiling. "Oh yeah, I see what you mean."

"But real life is more interesting. And," he said, looking directly into her eyes and speaking with the utmost clarity, "*your* life will *never* be boring." He said it with such an air of finality and authority that a chill went through her, and she wondered, *How could he know that?* Yet, there was something in the smugness of his smile that made her believe that somehow he did know.

"Well," she grumbled, "my life reads like a soap opera so far."

And for the next two hours Liz was surprised to find herself telling her new confidant about her failed love affairs, the tears, the pain, the self-condemnation, even her struggle with anorexia and her thoughts of suicide.

The young man listened patiently and non-judgmentally, never interrupting, just watching her with those eyes that seemed to peer into her soul. Liz felt as though a huge festering wound had been lanced, and the infection was draining away with every word. The release she sensed was indescribable.

Later, when Amber saw her and yelled down the hall, "Danfield! You missed dance class! What were you doing?" Liz smiled and replied, "Healing."

Amber didn't hear her, but she didn't pursue the subject. She shrugged and hurried away to catch up with a group of cast members from the musical, who were on their way to celebrate.

Liz walked back to her apartment, alone and strangely at peace.

Chapter Two

The dressing room was filled to capacity with the students in the Advanced Makeup class. Rows of bright lights framed every mirror, and photos of interesting faces, clipped from magazines for the students' "makeup morgues," were taped to the wall for reference. The dressing tables were strewn with pancake makeup, powder, lipsticks and eyeliners, oatmeal and cornmeal for texturing, rags, sponges, and various prostheses. The air smelled of latex and adhesive.

Most of the students wore bandannas to hold back their hair; some wore skullcaps and were busy masking the edges by fabricating wrinkles and blending colors. Some of the male students were creating hideous deformities for their faces, having chosen various monsters for their final projects.

Amber was wearing a wide, brightly colored long scarf, which had become her trademark, to hold back her short, black hair that had been dyed even blacker for emphasis. One could always see Amber coming, with her flamboyant dress and manner. She impressed a few, amused some, annoyed others, but it was hard to ignore her. Her makeup was usually applied in theatrical proportions—Amber's idea of glamour—but today she was in the process of transforming her young, smooth face into that of the hag whose picture hung by her mirror. She had just finished creating the bags under her eyes and was applying the adhesive to add a hooknose.

Next to her, Liz was forming foam latex into the shape of the cheeks and flat nose of a turtle and putting it onto the plaster casting of her own face that had been made in the fall. Around her neck a ring of nylon from a stocking drooped like the loose skin of a tortoise. The girls had been laughing about the picture Liz had clipped, and the similarity between the turtle's face and that of an elderly prof in the English department.

"You'd better watch it," Liz scolded. "If you don't give up smoking, this is what *you'll* look like!"

"Forget it, Danfield. I need my nicotine! Besides, I keep telling you, wrinkles are in the *genes*. Look at your turtle. He never smoked a cigarette!"

"He never wore jeans, either," Liz retorted. Then suddenly she changed the subject. "Hey, do you remember that guy that came to our table yesterday?"

"That crippled guy with the ponytail? Yeah." Amber said with a disagreeable expression.

"Did you hear him say what his name was?"

"Something that began with a J. I don't remember. He was too hard to understand, and I wasn't paying that much attention."

Yeah, I noticed, Liz thought with disgust. She was happy that she was meeting the young man for coffee again, but still embarrassed that all she knew was that his name began with a J. James? John? Joe? Jim? She supposed she could tell him the truth, that she had never heard what he said. Sure, why not? She had confessed much worse things than that the day before. She blushed to think how much of her life she had spilled out onto the table.

"I feel really embarrassed to tell you this, but I didn't hear you yesterday. What did you say your name was?"

The young man smiled, neither offended nor surprised. "It's J—"

Chapter Two

"*Omigosh*! I am *majorly* late!" A student at the next table jumped up with his books and bolted for the door, and once again Liz had missed the rest.

This is getting weird, she thought. *But I'm not going to ask him a fourth time!*

She smiled playfully. "Can I call you 'J'?"

He smiled back thoughtfully. "Sure. Yeah, I'd like that."

This time Liz kept an eye on the clock so as not to miss another class, but when it was time to go, she felt frustrated; she wanted to share so much more with J. She asked him if she could meet him after her last class and continue the conversation; he seemed delighted.

Their meetings became a daily habit, and it seemed they never ran out of things to talk about. Actually, Liz did most of the talking. J learned all about her childhood, growing up in an upper-middle-class family in the suburbs of St. Louis, her feelings of inferiority to her older sister Elaine, and how Liz had blossomed once Elaine had left home to pursue a lifestyle that caused her parents many sleepless nights.

J heard all about her acting career at the small private school she had attended, and how this brief period of theatrical success had sparked in her the desire to be an actress. And of course, J knew how that dream had slowly eroded away over four years in U of I's drama department. Here she was competing not with a dozen other girls, but with a hundred, and the scripts frequently contained a great deal of what Liz considered sleaze, rather than plays carefully selected by a protective private-school drama teacher.

Liz told him all about what she called the "caste system"—pun intended—in the drama department. According to her, there were still the cool people and the un-cool people, a social game that should have been obsolete past high school age. Whether this caste system existed in reality or in the insecurity of Liz's mind, he never questioned.

At the end of two weeks, J knew Liz's opinions on politics, theater, literature, films, and theories of the universe. He listened patiently, always interested, always giving her his undivided atten-

19

tion. When he finally spoke, his words were few, yet Liz had never known a man with so much wisdom. She wondered where he got it. Perhaps from a lifetime of struggle and rejection? Or did he get it from simply listening to people so attentively? She didn't know, and she wasn't sure she cared where he got it. She only knew this person, whose name began with a J, had fast become her confidant and closest friend. She became so relaxed around him that going back to the theater department and the rest of the world was beginning to seem like a chore. After an hour or two of being totally herself, she was finding it a pain to have to begin weighing words again according to the person to whom she was speaking, and the awareness, the self-consciousness of what she looked like. Sometimes, after confiding a deep hurt to J, she would sense the need to go and reapply the makeup she had cried off, and it occurred to her how nice it was to have a friend who didn't give a rip what she looked like, because he couldn't really tell anyway.

Liz wanted to be like J, seeing not the surface, but what was within. But as J had pointed out to her, her 20/20 vision could get in the way of really seeing. And her healthy, normal body naturally had a hard time sitting still and listening the way J did.

"That, and I'm too self-centered," Liz admitted one day. It seemed to her that she was the one who benefited the most from this relationship. J's words of insight always hit home, since he knew her so well by now, having studied her since day one.

Liz learned a few things about J, too. He was an only child, abandoned early in life by a father who couldn't deal with the fact that his son was so severely handicapped. His mother, now dead, had loved him dearly and had worked two full-time jobs: her paid job as a night nurse and the more important, more exhausting job of raising a child with cerebral palsy and very limited vision; it was the latter job to which she had been totally devoted. She had seen to it that he had received all the therapy he needed to reach his maximum potential physically, and at the same time she had recognized that this damaged child was bright and gifted. It had been she who had instilled in him the values he lived—the humility, kindness, and belief in the infinite worth of every person, includ-

Chapter Two

ing himself. And she had helped him find his calling; she had sacrificed deeply for his education, and J, having finally won a full scholarship, was now well on his way to becoming a psychologist. Liz was eternally grateful to J's mother. Although she had never met her, and never would, she was glad this woman had raised up for her this friend, dearer than a brother, with whom she could share anything and everything.

"Anything and everything" included Liz's writings. J always listened and gave her feedback that was honest, yet gentle. In this way he taught her not to take herself too seriously.

"Liz, you've written some magnificent poems!" he exclaimed on one occasion.

"You really think so?" she asked doubtfully.

"Oh, yes!" He paused, then added with a twinkle in his eye, "And that wasn't one of them." Liz blushed and stuck out her lower lip. The pout was short-lived, though; it's hard to sulk and snicker at the same time.

It felt good to laugh at herself. So good, in fact, that she went on to relate to him the somewhat embarrassing story of her experience with Les, the transfer student with whom she had spent a great deal of time at the beginning of the year. Les had always been friendly to her, and she had enjoyed his company immensely. He had never caused her to feel uncomfortable, unlike other male students, who always seemed to look at her as if she were a juicy piece of meat.

"Then one day, after an especially pleasant conversation with him, he had to rush off to class just as some sophomore girls were coming in. One said, '*Man*, he's gorgeous!' and the other one said, 'And he's so nice!' I had to agree. Then the first one said, 'Couldn't you just *cry*?' and the other one said, 'What a tragedy, such a waste!' And there I sat feeling like a total idiot, 'cause I'd never known—it never *occurred* to me—he wasn't 'into' girls! How embarrassing!" She covered her face with her hands.

"And disappointing," J added sympathetically.

"Yeah," Liz sighed. "How come there are so many gay guys in the theater?" She had come to think of J as someone who knew everything.

"People think they are who they think other people think they are."

"Uh . . . run that by me again?"

He smiled and spoke slowly. "People tend to become what they perceive others believe they are. For example, you have a little boy who loves to sing and dance and wear costumes. His dad tells him that's sissy stuff and that he should be out playing football. The boy gets older and he still would rather sing and dance and dress up than play football, and he thinks maybe he'd like to spend his life doing it. He starts hearing other terms besides 'sissy'—you know, the 'politically correct' nonsense. And he starts wondering if that's what he is. And, if his dad is still into the macho thing, the son might still be starved for male approval, which he confuses for love, and so he labels himself 'gay.' And he really believes that's what he is. That is, unless he goes into a totally different kind of denial and majors in law or medicine or whatever his dad wants him to do. Then he'll spend the rest of his life frustrated and not even know why."

"Wow! Did you learn that in the psych department?" Liz asked.

J smirked. "No way," he answered. "But I don't have to believe everything I'm told there. I learn much more just observing people, and I've seen—I've experienced—that people do become what others tell them they are. That's why I'm fortunate that my father left early. If I had spent my entire childhood listening to him tell me I would never amount to anything, I wouldn't be here. I'd be in an institution someplace, majoring in drooling."

"I'm glad you're here and not there."

"So'm I. Drooling's not my forte."

Liz laughed, then became thoughtful.

"I'm not sure what *my* parents are expecting. I don't think they'd mind so terribly much if I don't turn out to be an actress. I don't think they were too happy that I picked such a strange major anyway. I'm sure they'd rather I go into real estate or something else that fits more into St. Louis suburbia. But I also get the feeling, from my mother especially, that they're waiting for me to come home with a husband—or better yet, come home and marry one of their friends' sons. I'm afraid the way things are going, they're

Chapter Two

going to be disappointed in that, too. Maybe you could help me sort out what to do with my life after I graduate—you being a counselor and all."

"Well, I don't have my master's degree yet, you know."

"I know. I'm glad. I'd hate to think what I'd owe you if you were licensed and charging me by the hour!" Liz felt a little guilty at times that she took so much of J's time. Was she using him?

On the other hand, the thought crossed Liz's mind that perhaps J was just using her, for "practice" to be a counselor. These thoughts didn't come from anything he had said or done, but from her own feelings of low self-worth. When she was with him, in her heart she had no doubt that he really did care about her. He always treated her as though she were the most important person in the world. If people truly took on the identity they perceived from others, she thought, she wanted to spend as much time as she could with J. If she could become half as special as he seemed to think she was . . .

Liz was standing outside the theater office reading the bulletin board when a familiar voice behind her asked, "Can I help you?"

She turned to see one of her professors, who looked embarrassed as he stammered, "Liz! Excuse me, I didn't recognize you."

"No problem," she replied. It must have been her hair, she thought. She had lazily pulled it back into a barrette, rather than take the time to go through the ritual of curling, combing, spraying, and fretting.

"You OK, Liz?" Amber asked in speech class.

"Yeah, why?"

"You look a little pale's all—well, now you don't, you're blushing. Never mind."

Sheesh, thought Liz, rolling her eyes and taking out her script.

Walking across the quad that day, Liz felt that something was different. Ordinarily when she walked by, male heads would turn, and there was almost always at least one infantile jerk who would greet her in a way that made her uncomfortable. Today was refreshingly free from that sort of irritation, and she could think about more profound subjects uninterrupted until she met with Mike, another acting student, to practice a scene for dialects class.

Halfway through the first run-through, Mike commented, "There's something different about you today."

"The way I look, or the way I act?"

"I'm not sure. Maybe both. What is it?"

"Beats me," said Liz, but she was really beginning to wonder.

The only person who didn't treat her any differently that day was J. He listened to her chatter with the usual attentiveness and patience. He smiled as she recited her lines from the script she had been working on for dialects class, a scene from *No Exit*, which she was to perform with a French accent. She then told him about the argument that had broken out at a rehearsal for *Charlotte's Web* for the children's theater.

Jason Bryant, a somewhat diminutive member of the cool group, had just discovered that his costume for the part of Templeton included a papier-mâché headpiece. It was an oversized rat's head with an open space for breathing and speaking, and directly above that, a pair of papier-mâché buck teeth, which looked . . . well, rather un-cool. One of the stagehands made a crack having to do with Jason's manhood, and the resulting laughter from the others had encouraged the backstage comedian. He continued razzing the rat until Jason decided he'd had enough.

"But for once in his life, he was speechless—I mean, he was *so* mad and frustrated, he got totally tongue-tied! So finally he let out this scream of rage and rammed Greg right in the stomach with his head—or, rather, Templeton's head! And then"—Liz interrupted herself with little explosions of laughter—"there was a knock-down-drag-out fight! I guess Jason realized his bad timing right away. Not only is he about half Greg's size, but he still had on that ridiculous headpiece—every time he tried to get it off, Greg would push him down, and of course he could hardly see at all in it. So finally," she went on, almost breathless with giggles, "in desperation, he reached out, grabbed Greg by the ankle, and *bit* him! I

Chapter Two

mean, can you picture this—a five-foot-tall rodent in blue jeans with a papier-mâché head biting you on the ankle?"

J, who had somehow managed to keep a straight face, responded simply, "I *hate* it when that happens."

Liz blinked at him a moment and once again exploded into such uncontrollable laughter that tears were running down her cheeks. Guessing that by now she had mascara streaming down her face, she excused herself from the table.

In the ladies' room, the reflection in the mirror startled her. So *that* was why practically everyone had acted so strangely toward her that day. Besides skipping the hair ritual, she hadn't bothered (or remembered) to put on any makeup that morning. Her fair complexion looked very white in the fluorescent light, and the freckles she usually concealed with plenty of foundation were displayed for all to see. Without the striking auburn mane that usually framed it, such a pale face looked positively naked to her.

But while a month ago that sort of thing would have sent her into fits, today she wasn't really very concerned, and that realization made her wonder if she had become a little more like J. She entertained the thought for a moment, then admitted to herself as she hastily removed the barrette and applied her "face" that she hadn't quite arrived at that level of maturity yet. As she blended and powdered, the irony hit her: People spend so much money on vision tests, glasses, and contact lenses in order to see perfectly clearly, while women spend a small fortune trying to erase lines and freckles and blemishes and make their appearance more of a soft blur. *People are strange*, she observed, as she snapped her compact shut and ran her fingers through her long tresses.

As she walked back to her apartment that evening, Liz reflected on what it would feel like to be completely unshackled by public opinion, not to be forever wasting time and energy trying to impress people.

But impressions were what theater was all about. Impress your teacher, impress the director, impress the audience, impress each other; it was hard to know when to quit. The male students especially didn't seem to realize when the scene was over, blurring the line between make-believe and reality, and the most charming ones were the worst. J had told Liz once that the ancient Greek word for hypocrite meant, literally, "play-actor." She had laughed and quipped, "So I'm majoring in hypocrisy!"

If that were the case, she guessed she made a lousy hypocrite. Maybe that wasn't so bad.

"I think I'm the only one in the theater department who doesn't have a date for the cast party," Liz complained to J one day.

"Is that so bad?" J asked.

"It wouldn't be," she admitted, "if it weren't so typical. Everyone tells me how attractive I am, but I haven't had a date in over a year. What's the deal?"

"Maybe they're looking for something besides 'attractive.' You know, something perhaps you aren't willing to provide so freely?" J knew her well.

"Oh, I know that's true with a lot of them. The last date I had was a disaster." Liz went on to tell J about her one and only date with Wesley Matthews, the guy every girl in the theater department wanted to go out with. Wesley's idea of a good time and Liz's were not one and the same, and Liz, having been brought up to be polite, had tried to use tact to no avail, then to gracefully squirm out of the situation, and had finally resorted to slapping his face and making a quick exit. Wesley was not used to this kind of treatment and had been none too happy about it, and word had spread quickly that Liz was a prude.

"'Prude' is OK," J assured her. "Chastity's nothing to be ashamed of."

"Oh, I don't mind, I guess. I don't want to go out with that kind of guy anyway. But what about the nice ones? Even if they aren't as cute, I don't care. Heck, the *ugly* ones don't even ask me out!"

"Hey, I didn't know you wanted me to," J protested with mock defensiveness.

Liz stopped short, thinking she had to say something, but at a loss for words. But before she could mentally berate herself for all the ways she had probably offended him, he went on.

Chapter Two

"Liz, they're intimidated. For all their bravado, most guys are insecure. They see your beauty, and they figure right away you're out of their league. They don't see the kind person you are inside, because they don't get close enough to see. And even if they do," he added with a look of sadness in his eyes that Liz didn't discern, "the thought of your rejecting them is so painful, they don't dare risk it. So, they keep their distance, and some of them call you cruel names."

"Like 'stuck-up'?"

"Exactly."

"But the girls that put out they call 'sluts,' and if you put out just a little, they call you a 'tease.' You can't win!" Liz was exasperated. "What do guys want anyway?"

J shook his head. "Most of them don't know. And it makes them miserable. So, some take it out on sweet people like you. Others don't want to take it out on you, so they just leave you alone." J had a way of summing up things that Liz had spent years trying to figure out. She was glad his explanation didn't point to her as the problem.

"Well what about you? You aren't intimidated by me."

"I can't see you," he replied smugly.

Liz was looking at J instead of the coffee she was reaching for, and before she knew it, she had knocked the cup over, and coffee was dribbling off the side of the table. Her frustration came back in a hurry. As she grabbed for napkins, she blurted out angrily, "Oh, Liz, you *idiot!*"

"Hey!" J shouted, his voice full of fire as one fist hit the table.

Liz froze and her face went pale; she had never seen him angry before. Then her face went from white to red as she realized people were turning and looking at them. She slowly and timidly sat down, her eyes and J's locked, as coffee trickled off the table unchecked.

J spoke softly but intensely. "You're talking to someone I care about very much. And," he leaned forward until his face was inches from hers, "you *will not* talk to her that way!"

Liz sat wide-eyed for a moment, then humbly murmured, "Yes, sir."

In spite of having been thoroughly rebuked, she had a strangely gratifying sense of security. She had never had anyone defend her so zealously, and it was nice to know there was someone who would, even if it was against her own self-accusations.

Of course, she had no way of knowing what he had already saved her from, or the many ways in which he would defend her in the days to come.

Chapter Three

"Well, opening night's tonight," Liz told J. Not that he didn't know. J had listened to her stories of rehearsals, opinions of the director, complaints, plans, and descriptions of her costumes. As with every other aspect of the musical, Liz had mixed feelings about opening night.

"All the girls with the big parts get flowers and presents and little love notes and other nauseating stuff. All I'll get is the thrill of being crammed into one dressing room with the rest of the chorus. Oh well, it's better being one of the people dressing this time than one of the techies that have to clean up. Still, having to watch all the gift giving and mush, it'll be as bad as Valentine's Day. Man, I *hate* Valentine's Day . . ."

The dressing room was indeed crowded as the girls applied their makeup, donned their nun's habits, and paced the floor doing vocal warm-ups. Liz enjoyed getting ready, sitting in front of the lighted mirror, creating a formal coiffure to be unveiled later for the dinner party scene, and fantasizing that she had a big part. She tried to ignore the girls who were opening little gifts and cards and "break-a-leg" notes from their boyfriends; she didn't want to hear about it.

Counselor

A commotion at the dressing room door drew her attention away from her daydreams for a moment. Through the cluster of chorus members, she saw a young delivery boy, flustered by meeting such an abundance of feminine loveliness. He held a large floral box. *I don't want to know about it*, thought Liz, turning back to her mirror. Then she heard, "Liz Danfield?" She was certain she had heard wrong, until

"Oh, Li-i-iz!" sang a chorus of voices.

Stunned, Liz made her way to the door and took the box, so dazed that she forgot to thank the delivery boy. A couple of girls squealed, "Open it!" in unison. Off came the red ribbon, and as Liz lifted the lid, a gasp could be heard.

One dozen red roses. And a card, on which was written in a shaky hand,

> "Big parts are nice. Big hearts are better . . .
> You're a star, and I'm proud of you."

By the time Liz had read the note, she didn't have to read the signature to know who had sent it: "J."

Liz felt like a star that night, even in a nun's habit surrounded by other chorus members all singing the same songs. The audience was irrelevant to her, except for the man in the front row with a cane and thick glasses, listening attentively with a smile she knew was just for her.

A few days later, he was wearing that same smile as Liz approached the table where they were meeting. But the smile faded the moment she sat down, for although her casual manner had fooled everyone else that morning, she couldn't keep anything from him, even if she had wanted to. He knew something was troubling her, other than the usual post-performance letdown, and he wasted no time in small talk.

"You're hurting. Tell me about it." The tears she had held back until now began to spill over, and she fumbled in her purse for a tissue, which she didn't have. Gently J handed her his napkin, and she sniffled "Thanks."

Chapter Three

She began in a choked voice, "Well, today they posted the cast for *The Miser*, and three guesses who's *not* in it. It's the last play of the year, so I guess I'm an official failure."

"Failure?" J scolded. "You know better than that!"

"I know!" Liz quickly corrected herself, wanting to avoid another scene. "But I feel like one." Liz blew her nose, then sobbed, "I get A's in every scene in acting class, so why can't I get one lousy part in a play? What am I doing wrong?!"

J waited for her to calm down, and to ascertain whether this were a real question or just a release of pent-up frustration. When she repeated, quietly but seriously, "What am I doing wrong?" he looked at her fondly, took a deep breath, and said, "You majored in the wrong thing."

"Oh great! That's just what I want to hear six weeks before I graduate!" When Liz heard the sarcasm in her own voice, she stopped. It would do no good to alienate her closest friend by taking it out on him. Besides, he was the wisest person she knew; she should probably listen to him.

"I'm sorry," she said, dabbing her eyes. "What were you saying?"

"Liz, you're not an actress, you're a writer."

"A writer?"

"Of course. You love to do it, don't you?"

"Well, yes, but . . ."

"And you express yourself very well." He smiled. "I should know, right?"

Liz blushed. "Yeah, I talk your ear off every day."

"You've got a lot of thoughts going through that head of yours, and a lot of stories to tell. Instead of telling them all to me, why don't you write them down?"

Instead of?

"Can't I do both? I mean, I can't imagine *not* talking to you. I'd miss you."

Liz saw the look on J's face, and knew immediately that she had made him genuinely happy. It was a wonderful feeling. More than wonderful. After all he had done for her—the healing, the laughter, the encouragement—she realized that she wanted more than anything to make him happy. And after such a recent bitter disappointment, she was surprised by the sudden surge of satisfaction in knowing that she *could* make him happy. Now there was a gift worth having!

"I mean it," she said earnestly. "What would I do without you?" And she saw behind the thick lenses that tears of joy filled his eyes.

They were the most beautiful eyes she had ever seen.

Chapter Four

As spring brought the balmy weather at last, students could be seen all over campus, walking, studying, or dozing in the sunshine. As Liz walked to class, she could hear the music of the Beach Boys carried on the warm breeze through the window of a nearby apartment. She had heard their songs on her parents' stereo since she was a tot and now the young voices, singing familiar lines about sun and sand, and the admonition to let the teacher know they're surfin' were like heralds proclaiming the joyous news: "Summer's comin'!" Where a month before there had been snow, the grass on the quad was a rich green, and overhead delicate new leaves adorned the stately boughs of the huge oak and elm trees.

Later that afternoon under one of those trees sat a pair some of the students had dubbed Beauty and the Beast. Beauty had fair skin and long, auburn curls with highlights that shone like spun gold in the sunshine. The Beast was considerably less impressive; he had a small frame and slightly twisted arms with fingers that curled almost into a fist. He had a brace on his knee; Beauty had a guitar on hers. She was singing a ballad as her companion lay on the grass, his eyes closed with the contentment of listening to the sound of her voice. As she finished the song, he sighed with pleasure.

"I could listen to you all day."
"Careful, I could sing all day."
"Did you write that one?"
"Me? No! A friend taught it to me."
"What's this 'Me? No!' stuff?"
"I don't write songs."
"Why not?"
"Well, I . . . can't."
"Can't?"
"I mean, I never have."

He wasn't going to let her off that easily. "There's a first time for everything," he nagged.

She rolled her eyes and sighed. "I don't know," she mumbled, plucking absently at the strings.

He pulled himself up on one elbow and demanded, "Give me one good reason why you couldn't write songs!"

"I just . . ."
"Hey, you write poetry, don't you?"
"Yeah."
"And you play that thing, don't you?"
"It's called a guitar, J. Yes, I play."
"So . . ." he went on, giving a stirring motion with his hand, "put them together. All you need is a little inspiration."

She looked at this person who could hardly see her. "I think I've got that," she said quietly.

Satisfied, he flopped back on the grass. "Good, then it's settled. Write me a song."

She stared at him, intrigued at this new prospect. "OK, I will!" she said decisively. She played with a few chords, feeling the warm wind in her hair and the sunlight on her face. Suddenly she stopped playing, put her head back and laughed.

Though not knowing why, J laughed with her. "What now?" he inquired.

"I'm so glad I'm out here in the sunshine instead of in that stuffy, dark theater, rehearsing dances and drinking stale coffee!"

"Me too. I hate stale coffee and I'm a lousy dancer."

Chapter Four

The chimes in Altgeld Hall struck five.

"I do need to go in an hour, though," said Liz. "I have to go to the opera department for my last practicum."

"Which practicum is that?"

Liz had explained to J that theater majors had numerous courses to take, with a minimal number of credits for each one. And each semester every theater student was expected to perform some duty for a production, putting into practice what he or she had learned. The theater department called it "practicum;" the students called it "free labor."

"Makeup. I'm in charge of the girls' chorus for *Carmen*. Tonight's dress rehearsal. It shouldn't be any big deal, though, probably just basic makeup times ten. I'd like to just teach them how to do their own. Then I'll just set up, supervise, and clean up when it's over."

"How many performances?"

She took a deep breath. "Six! Plus two dress rehearsals. I guess the local people really go for opera."

"I could stand a little culture myself," said J. "Any tickets left?"

"I'm sure there are."

"You gotta be kidding," moaned Liz under her breath. She had just arrived at the dressing room for the girls' chorus and walked in to find the ten young singers she had to turn into Spanish ladies: two brunettes, a redhead, and seven fair-skinned blondes. By the makeup table was a large cardboard box full of supplies: ten bottles of tan body makeup, ten jars of "suntan" greasepaint, ten black eyeliners, ten tubes of mascara, ten red lipsticks, translucent powder, and three dozen cans of black, temporary-color hair spray.

"OK, you guys, listen up!" Liz spoke with authority in her voice. This was something unusual for her, but now that she was in the opera department with people she didn't know, who didn't know her, she had decided to take on a new role: the bossy makeup lady. She was surprised at her own boldness, but then, since meeting J a number of things were surprising her these days.

"I've got the dubious privilege of making you all look like sensuous senoritas." The girls giggled in unison. "First of all, they want you to arrive an hour before show-time, but until we get the hang of this—" the blonde locks practically created a glare "—better make it an hour and a *half*." Another chorus of giggles.

What followed was chaos. Liz showed the girls how to apply the tan body makeup to their arms and shoulders, but some of them had forgotten (or not heard) what she had told them about applying the translucent powder before dressing. The costume crew would not be happy about the white blouses smudged with tan that they would have to launder before the next performance. Excited chatter was interspersed with squeals of "This is so *gross*!" Black hair spray seemed to be everywhere, and the dressing room took on a certain characteristic fragrance that remained as long as "Carmen" did.

Finally the girls had been transformed into Carmen's companions from the cigarette factory, black-haired beauties in flowing skirts and white blouses positioned voluptuously off the shoulders. They lined up backstage to await their entrance, and Liz had the privilege of cleaning up the mess.

Then there was the long wait. Liz had made the mistake of signing up to work on an opera that turned out to be four hours long, and she realized that this was probably the reason the sign-up sheet had had so few names on it. Once the dressing room was tidied up, Liz had to wait through two acts before transforming the chorus into older women for a later scene. It was a hurry-up-and-wait activity: a mad dash to get everyone on stage, followed by two and a half hours of "hanging out," a fifteen-minute intermission in which to add thirty years to the appearance of ten young women, then another hour of waiting before cleaning up after ten girls who eagerly showered and washed the black out of their hair, leaving a trail of smudged towels in their wake.

Liz was permitted to sit in the audience during dress rehearsals, but after that she was going to have to wait backstage. That was fine with her; eight hours of Bizet was enough. The second night she visited another dressing room, where two techies were waiting for a scene change, hoping for a little light conversation. But the way one of the young men looked at her gave her an uneasy feeling and, after a remark that was no doubt meant to be

Chapter Four

charmingly funny but came across as downright crude, she returned to her post, resolving to bring a fat book to read during future performances.

It was past midnight when Liz made one last inspection of the dressing room before turning out the light and locking the door. Her footsteps echoed through the deserted hallway. Even though this was the fourth night of performances, she still felt nervous as she headed for the exit. In spite of the presence of campus security, she didn't like having to walk home alone.

As she pushed open the heavy glass doors, a voice made her fairly jump out of her skin.

"Buenos noches, senorita!" She started to scream and clapped her hand over her mouth.

"Are you trying to give me a heart attack?" she hissed.

"Sorry," said J. "I just thought you might want company walking home. After all," he added, taking her arm as he limped beside her, "you never know what kind of unsavory characters are at large. You might be glad to have a big strong man along for protection."

Although her heart was still pounding from the sudden scare, Liz smirked. "Sure would. You know any?"

"At your service!" he replied with a flourish. "I can protect you from any and all predators!" He flourished his cane in the air like a *Star Wars* light saber. "Just tell me where they are." He gave the air a thrust. "Hey, that was a pretty good opera."

"You were there? Where were you?"

"In the balcony. I got a better view from there. Good makeup job, lady."

"Yeah, right. How'd you get in?"

"I just turned on the old charm. The lady was a sucker for my good looks—at least I *think* it was a lady."

Liz chuckled and shook her head in amazement. *I don't believe this guy.*

"One question, though. How come all those Spanish people were singing in French?"

"It's Bizet."

"It's bi*zarre*, if you ask me."

Counselor

"Well, if it ain't Beauty and the Beast!" A voice, uncomfortably close, startled Liz. She looked up to see three tall young men who seemed to have appeared out of nowhere. She could tell they were students by their dress—the usual jeans, sweatshirts, and Nikes. She could also tell they were drunk by their subtle sway and the thickness of the one's speech. She was disturbed to see that the one in the middle was Wesley Matthews. She held her breath. Maybe in the dim moonlight he wouldn't recognize her.

No such luck.

"Hey, she's the one I told you guys about—the frigid one!" he announced loudly. Liz could feel the blood rising to her face.

"So, it *ain't* Beauty and the Beast," the biggest one sneered. "It's Frosty and the Freak!" The others guffawed loudly, as though this were the cleverest joke in the history of comedy. Liz's heart began to pound with the growing realization of her predicament. She tried to continue walking, but Wesley blocked their way.

"Yeah, Frosty. You thought you were too good for me, didn't you?" he demanded. His face was close enough to Liz's that she could see the glazed look in his eyes and smell the alcohol on his breath. He glared at J. "But you're not too good for this . . . *freak*!" He kicked J's cane out of his hand, nearly falling over as he did so. Ironically, J stood unshaken. As the cane clattered across the cobblestones and Wesley regained his balance, Liz's jaw tightened in resentment. She wanted to tell him off, but as the three of them towered over her now, quite literally breathing down her neck, she found herself too frightened to speak. She clutched J's arm more tightly, although she realized the absurdity of doing so; she could probably protect him better than he could her.

Her fear was fast turning to panic as Wesley, fists clenching and unclenching with an irrational rage, put his face up to J's. Liz winced, anticipating a blow but, oddly, Wesley seemed unable to lift his fist any higher. She could see the tension in his face increasing as a vein began to bulge in the middle of his forehead. With what seemed like the utmost frustration, he vented his anger, apparently in the only way he could.

"Freak!" he jeered. "Yeah . . . yeah," he stammered, "that's what you are, a . . . a freak . . . *Freak!* . . . *FREAK!*" he spat the word

Chapter Four

repeatedly, and he seemed to grow as he did. Pulling himself up to his full height, he seemed twice J's size, and Liz wondered what Wesley would do to him.

And then what would he do to *her*?

Of all of them, surprisingly, J was the only one who seemed calm. He slowly took off his moistened glasses and looked directly at Wesley. The others froze, watching intently. Wesley stopped shouting and stared back. At first his eyes registered blind hatred. Then he appeared to see something that struck terror into him. And, as the five stood there in the silent street with only the sound of their own breathing, Liz couldn't believe what happened next.

All three would-be assailants backed one step away from J, eyes locked with his. Then J finally spoke, not loudly, but firmly, one word.

"Go."

The countenances of the three had changed completely. Utterly intimidated, they turned, and without a word, they staggered away. Liz was dumbfounded.

J wiped his glasses with the corner of his shirt. As Liz stood there, frozen in astonishment, he limped over to pick up his cane, and a moment later he was offering Liz his arm. "Shall we go?" he asked pleasantly. She was still shaking and staring in the direction the intruders had retreated.

"How did you do that?" she gasped in amazement. J gave her that endearingly smug smile and answered her, again in one word.

"Authority."

They walked the rest of the way to Liz's apartment in silence.

Chapter Five

"Are you Liz?" a stranger's voice asked at the Commons. Liz looked up to see a friendly face with blue eyes, freckles, and a wispy beard.

"Yes?"

"I'm J's roommate, Gavin." Liz was a little surprised that the young man also called her friend "J." Apparently her nickname for him had stuck. But she didn't comment, just looked at him expectantly.

"He asked me to tell you he won't be here today. He's got the flu."

"Oh really?" Liz was genuinely disappointed, and sympathetic. "Can I do anything—make him some chicken soup or something?"

The young man chuckled and Liz noticed a dimple showing through his thin beard. "I don't think he wants soup, or *anything* to eat, if you know what I mean." He put his hand to his stomach and made a sour face.

"Oh, *that* kind of flu. Poor guy." It didn't seem fair. Wasn't it bad enough to have CP and be blind—not to mention the daily rejection—and now to have to endure that . . . stuff. When J had said he was "familiar with" suffering, he wasn't kidding.

"Oh, well," said Gavin, "at least it's what they call the twenty-four-hour flu. He should be better by tomorrow. He said to tell you he'll probably be here then."

"Thanks, Gavin," Liz smiled. She started to return to her book, but noticed that Gavin didn't go away. He stood looking as though he had something else to say, but all Liz heard was the blend of voices and rattling dishes. She looked up. "Would you like to sit down?" she asked.

"Uh . . . sure, OK." Gavin pulled up a chair and sat, never taking his eyes off Liz. She felt she should say something.

"So . . . he's your roommate?"

"Yep. My roommate and my buddy." He smiled, "And, he's kind of my counselor, too."

"I know what you mean," said Liz, missing him already. "He makes a great mentor, doesn't he?"

"He's told me a lot about you. He thinks you're pretty special." Liz smiled and blushed. The young man paused again, and a group of students on the other side of the cafeteria could be heard debating a hot topic. "Actually, he thinks you're more than special. He . . ." Gavin paused, as if weighing the risk of telling her something. "How special is he to you?" he asked.

Liz was caught off guard by this odd question. Then she saw in Gavin's blue eyes a real concern for his friend. "Very special," she said earnestly. "He's like a dear brother to me. I don't know how I would have survived this year without him. He's my best friend."

"Really?" asked Gavin, fascinated. "Why?"

Again a strange question. "I think you know why. You said yourself how great he is." She saw by his face that he wanted to hear more. OK, she'd tell him more. "He's the perfect person to be a counselor, isn't he? I mean, he listens, he understands, he cares. He's helped me see things in myself I didn't know were there, and when I've had problems, he's shown me how to find the solutions myself. He's a great . . . counselor," she repeated, for lack of a better word.

"I agree." Gavin seemed to be grasping for something. There was more to be said, and he finally said it.

"He loves you, Liz."

Chapter Five

What kind of an air-head does he think I am? she thought. "I know. I love him, too."

"But how much?" Gavin persisted. Liz was getting annoyed. "What do you mean?"

"I mean, do you love him enough to . . ." Finally he blurted it out. "You know, he wants to marry you."

Liz sat stunned. At the same time she wondered why the thought had never occurred to her until now. Maybe she *was* an air-head.

"Really?" she asked with dead seriousness. Gavin looked guilty.

"Please don't tell him I said anything!" he said hastily.

Liz paused for a moment; it was all still sinking in. "If that's true, why hasn't he said anything to *me* about it?" she asked suspiciously.

Gavin seemed irritated, as though the answer should have been obvious. "Your friendship means too much to him. If he were to ask, that would be the end of it." Then, seeing Liz's puzzled expression, he sighed and added, "He's assuming you'd say no."

Assuming I'd say no? Although the thought of marriage had not occurred to her as a possibility, it had never crossed her mind as an *impossibility* either. Now for the first time she was considering it.

"Why would he assume I'd say no?" she asked cautiously.

Gavin took a good look at Liz. Again. "Well look at you, you're . . . beautiful." Liz didn't interrupt; J had taught her not to deny the truth. "The good-looking women always end up with the good-looking men." His voice had a hint of bitterness in it, and Liz wondered for a moment what unhappy experience had brought him to that conclusion.

"Says who?" she snapped defensively, resenting the implication that she was somehow shallow and typical. Then she checked herself and decided that he hadn't meant to insult her. "I mean, that's not always the case."

"Look around you, Liz. The good-looking girls all want to marry good-looking guys. You know that."

"Good-looking guys! Now *there's* a quality to base a lifetime commitment on!" she declared sarcastically.

Then the thought hit her—*lifetime commitment*? Could she spend a lifetime with J? She thought of everything she had shared with him. The details of her life, the disappointments, the fears and insecurities, the dreams—J knew them all. He was the only one she had ever read her journal to, probably the only one who was interested. Could she spend the rest of her life with this kind of relationship?

She could think of nothing more natural.

She thought of marriages she knew that were based on impressions, on superficial traits that changed with the passing of time. How many marriages had split up because one partner had aged a little more gracefully than the other and had decided to trade his partner in for a younger, more attractive model? How many marriages ended even sooner because once the vows were said, the facade came down and the two learned for the first time just who it was that they had married?

Could she spend the rest of her life with someone who didn't know for sure, and certainly didn't care, what she looked like, and yet who knew her probably better than she knew herself—who knew every flaw and loved her with all his heart anyway? Could she spend the rest of her life with someone who recognized her gifts and encouraged her to be all she could be?

She could think of nothing more satisfying.

Liz was becoming overwhelmed by a feeling like an earthquake from within and something equally powerful from without—was it God?—telling her, *This is right!* As she sensed a growing resolve that she knew J had played a big part in teaching her, she looked Gavin directly in the eye and said with quiet intensity,

"You tell him I said yes."

She half expected that sick feeling that said *What did you get yourself into this time?* But it never came. Instead, it seemed that heaven itself was cheering. Her face was beaming, but the young man across the table from her sat bewildered, his mouth agape in astonishment.

"Do you realize what you're getting yourself into?" asked J. Liz noticed his hands were shaking; she reached across the table and gave them a squeeze.

Chapter Five

"Probably not," she confessed. "But then, what bride does? I probably know more than most." She eyed him with exaggerated suspicion. "Why? Are you hiding some deep dark secret?"

He stared back seriously. "Well, actually . . ." he paused for effect. "I'm really Arnold Schwarzenegger." Liz suppressed a smile.

"I knew that," she said defensively. "Anything else?"

"Besides my alien grandparents? No." He grinned mischievously at her for a moment. Then his smile faded. "I mean it, Liz. You know you're making a commitment to give up certain things . . . forever."

She sensed the serious turn the conversation was taking and felt this was one of those times to listen for a while and avail herself of J's wisdom. "Tell me," she said quietly.

"Liz, are you prepared to be my wife?"

"Didn't I just say I'd marry you?"

"But are you ready to be *my wife*? Are you willing to be *identified* with me for the rest of your life? If so, you can say good-bye to any thoughts of impressing the world or being popular. Someone like me doesn't get invited to many parties. I make people uncomfortable, and nobody comes to a party to be uncomfortable."

Liz thought of parties she had been to. She saw a mental image of food and drink and music and laughter and flirting—and drunkenness and lies and drugs. *OK, no parties. No problem.*

"In fact, we probably won't be welcome in any of the places the 'beautiful people' go. They may come to me for counseling behind closed doors when they run into a crisis, but most people will never acknowledge me publicly as a friend. And when all seems well, they will not even acknowledge my existence." He said this without self-pity, merely as if he were stating a fact he wanted to be sure she understood.

"That's their problem," Liz said stubbornly.

"Yes. It is," J went on. "I don't have that many friends, Liz, and neither will you. And we won't be wealthy. I'm not going to be one of those shrinks that charge an arm and a leg. Then people would just be exchanging their psychoses for bankruptcy. I want to be available to anyone who needs me. Does that disappoint you?"

"No, and it doesn't surprise me, either."

"Liz, if you become my wife, you may get *nothing* out of it except our relationship. So, I'm asking you, if that turns out to be the case, is our relationship enough?"

Liz tried to feel sober about all this as she thought hard about what she'd be giving up. A picture flashed through her mind—her dream of showing up at her high school reunion on the arm of the most gorgeous and wealthy man there, the envy of every girl who had ever snubbed her and called her a dweeb. Revenge would have been sweet, but to exchange a lifetime with her best friend for one evening of revenge? That was no bargain. She knew she was making a huge commitment, to someone she had known only a few months, and she tried to weigh the pros and cons—to be "realistic." But she couldn't stop the relentless tidal wave of joy that seemed to come from heaven itself, and that still, small voice telling her, *This is right!*

"Yes," she replied decisively, "it's enough. You're all I need."

Chapter Six

"Elizabeth Ann Danfield, Have you lost your mind?!"

Well, so far this "discussion" with her parents had opened up old wounds, reduced her status back to little girl, threatened to drive her back to her former eating disorder, and now questioned her sanity.

In short, it was going about the way Liz had expected.

"Mom, you haven't even met him."

"Honey,"—Liz could tell by her mother's tone of voice that a speech was coming—"I don't know why you would feel so guilty that you feel you must *punish* yourself by . . ."

"Don't psychoanalyze me, Mom. You know I detest it when you do that!"

Why was it that when she was with her parents she started using words like "detest"?

Liz's mother started to react, but her father touched her arm and said quietly, "Now Rachel, let's hear her out." Sensing the amount of tension that had built already, he took a deep breath and turned to Liz.

"Honey, let's start over. Tell us about this young man."

Liz's face relaxed somewhat, and she slowly took a breath. "He's a graduate student in the psychology department, and when he gets his degree he's going to be a psychologist." She paused to see whether her parents were impressed yet. "He's a great counselor already. He's counseled me so much just as a friend . . . He's my *best* friend, Dad. I can talk to him about anything at all, and he always, *always* listens, without interrupting. He—"

Rachel interrupted. "So you're marrying him because he's a good listener!" Liz didn't know whether the sarcasm she sensed was a product of her own defensive imagination, but before she could gain control, she blurted out,

"He *is* a good listener! Do you have any idea what a rare quality that is in a man?" There was a pause, and Liz was reasonably sure that they were all having the same mental picture, that of her father, George Montgomery Danfield, sitting in his easy chair, holding the newspaper in one hand and the remote in the other. After a moment of awkward silence, George decided to change the subject.

"What else do you like about him, honey?" He gave her a wink. "Is he good-looking?"

"Frankly, no." Liz smiled serenely. "And I don't care. And he doesn't care what I look like, either."

"No, I guess he wouldn't, being blind," Rachel muttered wryly. "And you want to spend the rest of your life with a blind man?"

"Mom, blind people can see a lot more than you think they can. In some ways more than we can."

"Very poetic, dear."

Liz flushed in anger at her mother's condescending tone of voice.

"But," her father finally spoke, mainly to change the subject. "You say he's a graduate student?"

"Yes, Dad. He graduated *summa cum laude*." Liz's voice was proud.

"I thought those people with muscular dystrophy were . . . well . . . slow."

Liz sighed. "It's cerebral palsy, Dad, and not all of them are mentally retarded. Some are normal mentally, some above normal."

"So this young man of yours is . . ."

Chapter Six

"Brilliant!" Liz boasted.

Her father seemed to be weighing the pros and cons. "But, he's still . . . handicapped."

Liz thought of her mother's moods, her father's absentmindedness, her own insecurities, and asked, "Aren't we all?"

Her mother, deflated, replied, "Touché, dear."

After another moment of silence, Liz's father said with exaggerated cheerfulness, "So! When do we get to meet him?"

Liz beamed. "How about this afternoon?"

Her parents looked at each other a moment, then said simultaneously, "Sure." Both of them still seemed very *unsure*. As she saw their bewildered expressions, thinking of all they had already been through with Elaine's rebellion, she felt a surge of compassion and affection. "I know you want the best for me, and I love you for it. Believe me, I've found the best."

"I hope so, darling," said Rachel with tears in her eyes.

Liz put an arm around each one of them and drew them close. The next moment she was startled to find herself hugging her pillow.

Chapter Seven

A dream? How much of it had been a dream? Just the conversation with her parents? She was still engaged to . . . to . . . his name began with a J.

She was struck by the absurdity of the thought. Of course she wouldn't be engaged to someone and not even know his name!

But she still had a friend who . . . didn't she?

Liz's mind was in a fog, as she tried to separate dream from reality. She was in her apartment near the campus, so she was still at school. She looked out the window to see a drab, gray morning. The ground was splotched with patches of snow; the trees were bare.

"So much for spring," she muttered. By now her thoughts were spinning as she absently dressed and brushed her hair. What if there were no J? But there *had* to be! He was her dearest friend! He knew everything about her! He was so real—wasn't he?

Then why didn't she know his name?

Why couldn't she picture his face?

As the dream began fading, her mind tried to grasp at the bits and pieces as they slipped away, but she might as well have been trying to catch a beam of light in the dark. Any image of her friend was soon gone, along with specific words of wisdom he had spoken. All that was left was a longing to be with him again.

"This is crazy," Liz told herself out loud. She opened the apartment door and picked up the morning paper. As she closed the door to the cold dampness, she checked the date: March 7. She checked the kitchen clock. She had plenty of time, but she began her morning routine with a sense of urgency. Make the coffee, grab some toast, pour some juice, find the creamer . . . as if enough activity would erase the dream and return her to what she considered sanity.

It didn't.

"You okay, Liz?" Amber asked in speech class.

"Uh, yeah, why?"

"You seem a little out of it today."

"Oh. Well . . . I didn't sleep too well last night."

Liz did more doodling than note-taking that period. Amber peered over at her notebook and spotted an ornate "J" in the margin. *Aha!* she thought. *Liz is in love!*

"Who's 'J'?" Amber asked after class with the look of a hungry gossip.

"I don't know," Liz answered defensively. It was true. Well, partially. How could she tell anyone she was in love with a man she had met in a dream? Especially one with less than average looks and multiple handicaps? She didn't understand it herself.

"OK, don't tell me!" Amber retorted, adding in a teasing voice, "I'll find out sooner or later." Then she was off to her next class.

"When you find out, fill me in." Liz muttered.

Liz had a strong sense of déjà vu as she stood outside the office with the other students waiting for the posting of the cast for the spring musical.

"You nervous?" a freshman asked her.

"Not really," Liz answered.

"I think you're going to get Leisl. I saw you try out. You're perfect for her."

Chapter Seven

"Thanks," Liz replied absently. Actually, she had never been so un-nervous about audition results before. Perhaps it was because she was reconsidering whether theater was really her calling. She didn't seem to fit, and at times it seemed so . . . fake. And, there were other things she liked to do. Like writing. She loved to write.

Then there was the familiar click of the door, the stage manager with the much-awaited piece of paper, the parting of the Red Sea, etc., etc. The ritual flowed on, with Liz feeling strangely detached from it all.

There were the hugs and squeals . . . *been there, done that.* Liz started to walk away without even looking at the list.

"Congratulations!" called a freckled student with sandy hair and a friendly smile. "You got it! You're Leisl!"

"What! I am?" Liz snapped back to reality. "Are you sure?"

"I'm the stage manager, I oughta know these things." The young man laughed. "Congratulations!" he repeated, giving her a wink and thumbs up.

"Thanks, Sean," she answered breathlessly as she made her way to the list to make sure he wasn't joking. There was her name, as she had so often dreamed it would appear.

"Oh, wow," Liz gasped, quickly heading for the door. "Wait til I tell—" her expression fell. "I . . . I've got to go call my parents and tell them." And she hurried to get away from the crowd.

Her parents were delighted and immediately got the dates of the shows so they could make arrangements to come and see their daughter's theatrical debut at the university. After hanging up, Liz felt a let-down; the thrill was over quickly. Now that she had told her parents, there was no one else to tell. Everyone in the theater department knew, and practically every acting major had been there, done that. Besides, most of them were too wrapped up in their own fragile egos to spend time discussing life with a late bloomer.

I feel like I'm hearing Christmas carols in January, she thought. There was a time when the thought of having landed a major role would have given her a surge of joy. But now, it was somehow too late.

I'm hearing Beach Boys songs in September, she thought. She felt a slight satisfaction at having found the right metaphor, but it was short-lived as she realized that there was really no one that she would be sharing it with.

As she approached the heavy doors, she stopped to zip up her jacket. The cold, damp wind made her feel even more alone and vulnerable, but at least the occasional raindrop hitting her face would camouflage any tears. Her makeup instructor had always said, "If you can't hide something, just add something else—confuse the issue."

Slowly, somehow suddenly tired, Liz walked back to her apartment, missing someone, who for all she knew, didn't exist.

Chapter Eight

Although Liz had lived in Urbana-Champaign for nearly four years, she had never been inside Carle Hospital until today. As she found her way to the physical therapy room, she wondered what exactly she would say to her former roommate, Sarah Emmons. Sarah was a biology major who aspired to becoming a physical therapist. In the meantime she had volunteered to help out at the hospital.

"Hey, Liz!" Liz was greeted by a petite brunette with flawless, cream-colored skin. While her classmates basked in the sun, "working on their tans," Sarah spent every free hour here beneath the fluorescent lights, bringing her own brand of sunshine to a few individuals who badly needed it. She made her way over to Liz and gave her a hearty hug.

"How are ya?" Although her pink, volunteer's uniform was simple, her jewelry confined to a tiny gold cross around her neck, she seemed radiant. Her blue eyes sparkled with a joy that was enviable.

Liz peered in curiously at the room full of equipment, where therapists were working with patients in conditions ranging from sports injuries to serious disabilities. What a contrast to the theater, Liz thought. She was used to artificial settings painted on flats or backdrops, and memorized lines of fictitious characters that covered over real situations that nobody wanted to confront. But here was the "real world," with problems that could not be ignored, and Sarah confronted them with an unrelenting cheerfulness that assaulted the darkness like the sun; she had certainly found her niche.

"So, how *are* ya?" she repeated. "What's new in the wonderful world of the theater?"

"I got a major part in the spring musical, that's real new!" Liz laughed.

"No kidding!" Sarah exclaimed with genuine excitement. "That's *great!* What musical?"

"*The Sound of Music.*"

"I *love* that one! So who are you gonna be?"

"Leisl, the—"

"—eldest daughter. Wow! So you'll have a solo and everything!"

Liz smiled. Sarah seemed more excited than she was. Liz said, "Yep . . ."

"'Sixteen, Going on Seventeen'?" Sarah guessed, grinning. "So when is it?"

"Late April. It'll be posted all over campus. Come, OK?"

"Are you kidding? I wouldn't miss it! I'm so happy for you!" Sarah gave Liz another hug, something Liz just now realized she had been needing. "So, what are you doing in my neck of the woods?"

"Oh," Liz tried to sound casual. "I was thinking about you and I thought I'd drop by to say hi. It's been a while."

"Sure has. It's good to see you! You want to go to the cafeteria and get some coffee?"

"Oh, that's OK. I'd kinda like to see where you work." *This is crazy*, Liz thought. *I don't know what would make me think that . . .*

"Well, this is it," Sarah said with a theatrical gesture. "Welcome to my world."

"Do you work with a lot of patients?" Liz asked, her eyes scanning the room.

Chapter Eight

"Depends on what you mean by 'a lot.' At the moment there are about ten. Some require more work than others. Some of the hospital patients are in several times a day, some outpatients come in three times a week."

"So . . . do you get to know them pretty well?"

"Oh, yeah, some of them. Especially the ones that are in several times a day," she laughed, rolling her eyes. "You get to know their attitudes. Everybody's got a different attitude."

"What kinds of problems do they have?" Liz asked in a low voice, hoping none of the patients could hear her.

"Oh, stroke, accidents, birth defects, all kinds of things."

"Birth defects? Like cerebral palsy?"

"Yeah, as a matter of fact there's one of them. Joey over there has CP." Liz snapped to attention and looked in the direction Sarah had indicated. A toddler lay on a table while three volunteers were moving his arms, legs, and head. Her heart sank. She sighed. Then noticing that Sarah was looking at her with a puzzled expression, she tried not to appear disappointed.

"What are they doing?" she asked casually

"It's called 'patterning.' Kids with CP . . . you might say they're missing certain connections in the brain. They have a hard time coordinating their arms and legs like normal babies do when they learn to crawl and walk. In CP babies it takes a lot more repetition to make that connection, so in patterning the volunteers do it for him. They repeat the motion over and over for about five minutes at a time. It's not difficult or complicated, but it has to be done several times a day, and it takes at least three people."

"At least?"

"You need one to turn the head from side to side, and one for each side to move the arms and legs in a crawling motion. But sometimes there's one person for each arm, and one person does both feet. It just depends on how many people are here. And how cooperative the patient is. As long as the motion is coordinated and rhythmic, hopefully the brain makes the connections sooner or later, so he'll be able to crawl on his own."

"I never knew learning to crawl was so complicated," Liz commented.

"We take a lot for granted, that's for sure. The brain is an incredible creation." Sarah shook her head in amazement. "And some people think it evolved by chance!" she added, as though it were the craziest idea anyone had ever come up with. *Here we go*, thought Liz. *Jo's always trying to bring God into every conversation.* She didn't take the bait, but continued to watch the volunteers and the submissive little boy.

"He's pretty patient about it."

"He's in a good mood today. Sometimes he fusses. Sometimes he *screams*! I guess you gotta let him have his moods like any normal kid."

"Any adults? With CP, I mean." Liz tried to sound nonchalant.

"No, we haven't had any adults here with CP. Therapy for CP is usually done when they're kids."

"Oh," Liz murmured absently. Then she casually asked, "Do you *know* any adults with CP?" Sarah continued to look at her quizzically, so she added, "I . . . think I may know someone with that."

Sarah paused to think. "No, I don't think I've ever . . . wait, yes, I do. McDaniel . . . Jerry."

Liz tried to conceal her excitement as she asked, "Would that be Jerry with a J?"

Sarah seemed caught off guard. "Gee, I don't know, I only met the guy once. His wife was in one of my biology classes a couple of years ago. Nice lady . . . but I didn't know her that well." Sarah's face was now one big question mark. "Would that be the person you know?"

"I don't think so." Trying to re-establish some impression of normalcy, Liz added with exaggerated enthusiasm, "Hey, on second thought, I think I *would* like to go for coffee."

"Could we go to the cafeteria, Mrs. B?" Sarah asked a motherly looking woman who was apparently the head of the department. She smiled at the girls.

Chapter Eight

"Go ahead, Sarah, take your time, we've got plenty of help today. Must be the rain." Sarah smiled knowingly; when the weather was beautiful, she was often the only one to show up.

"Let's go, Liz. I want to hear all about your upcoming stardom!"

Stardom. Now that Liz had at long last gained a foothold in the theater, a goal she had so long pursued, she was unsure whether this career was really what she wanted. This new ambiguity was maddening. The idea of climbing up the ladder of success only to find it leaning against the wrong wall sounds humorous only when it happens to someone else. As little as Liz could recall of her dream about her mysterious friend, one thing she remembered: she had made a commitment, and she was sticking to it. She had realized that she couldn't have everything, but that had been OK; she'd recognized what was most important to her and was willing to abandon anything and everything else. It had been a wonderful feeling, finally knowing the direction her life was going, and being totally devoted to one thing—or in this case, one person.

But, now that the mirage had evaporated, Liz couldn't look far into the future without the same old uncertainty and indecision. Seeing Elaine's disastrous life from a distance had taught her a great deal about making bad choices, but it had also made her fearful about major decisions in general. What if she were to make the wrong choice? Being a perfectionist, she wanted to see her life all neatly planned and mapped out before her, and it just wasn't happening. And, being the perfectionist, she also wanted to avoid anything that stirred up her emotions too much, lest she make some rash decision that would ruin her. So, although she loathed herself for being so cowardly, she found that the best way to cope with life at the moment was to focus her attention on the here and now. And the intensity of college life, especially the theater, can make that very easy to do.

Liz was kept very busy the next few weeks, juggling her studies and rehearsals. Homework got done between classes, lines for the play studied over lunch. At five o'clock scarcely out of class for the day, she had barely an hour to grab something to eat before rehearsal started.

She always arrived at the Commons at the busiest, noisiest time of day, so she always opted for dinner "to go." Standing impatiently in line with the other harried students, Liz would see the ones who had more time sitting at tables sharing a laugh or debating the issues of the day, their animated voices echoing camaraderie and controversy over the clatter of dishes. It was common to see extra chairs squeezed together around an overloaded table, and boisterous students exploding in periodic bursts of laughter. Occasionally she'd see a couple in the crowd quietly talking eye to eye, apparently wrapped up in more personal matters, sometimes holding hands, sometimes smiling as if sharing an unspoken secret.

No time for that sort of thing now, she'd remind herself, *now that I'm a "star."* The idea still amused her. She sighed. *I guess it's just as well that . . .*

"Three seventy-eight, please." The routine voice snapped her back to business before any emotion could set in.

"OK."

Then it was hand the lady the money, get change, stuff sandwich in backpack, put on hat, grab drink, head back to Krannert, eat and study lines, meet with costume crew for measurements, get to music room for warm-ups, hurry, hurry, hurry . . . By the time rehearsal was over and Liz got back to her apartment, it would be late. And by the time she had finished the remainder of her studying for the next day it would be even later, and Liz would collapse into bed, involuntarily running lines in her head until she fell into a deep, deep sleep, seemingly without dreams.

Liz had much to occupy her thoughts, though seldom the opportunity for any serious reflection. But on those rare occasions when she had time to breathe she would seize moments to record sparks of insight in her journal. It was then that she would sense a certain presence, as though an interested observer were watching over her shoulder.

She hadn't yet dared to write anything in her journal about him, that friend known to her only in a dream, whose name began with a J, whose face she couldn't remember, yet whose presence

Chapter Eight

she couldn't forget. And she couldn't shake the feeling that somehow this person was real, and that he was, at that moment, very close.

Chapter Nine

When spring vacation came, it was a relief for Liz to have a break from the university rat race and get home for some R & R with her doting parents. Rachel Danfield tearfully fretted over how thin her daughter looked and hit the kitchen with renewed ambition, preparing feasts that would satisfy both the pickiest gourmet and the heartiest glutton. Meanwhile, George, as usual, wanted to take her out to lunch and "show her his office." It amused Liz that her father always wanted to show her where he worked. This he had done regularly since as a tiny child she had first asked him, "What do you do, Daddy?" Long before "Take Your Daughter To Work Day" was ever heard of, George was introducing her to his colleagues, the secretaries, the janitors, the customers. It was obvious that while he was showing his daughter the office, he was much more interested in showing the office his daughter. Though this ritual embarrassed Liz at times, it also made her feel secure to know that Daddy was proud of her.

Liz enjoyed the luxury of the queen-size bed in her room and sleeping in every morning. Her body soaked up the rest like a thirsty sponge, and the familiar home-cooked meals her mother fussed over every night were a welcome and nostalgic change from the nightly subs at school. It was heaven to lounge in the La-Z-Boy, being able to read—not study, just read—the comics, a magazine, a cheap novel.

The Galleria, Liz's favorite mall, was an almost forgotten delight, and she gazed at the store windows like a child at Christmas. It was great to unwind—and spend money. Her mother was very good at that. After a morning of trying on dresses and shoes, sampling chocolates at the candy counter, strolling through the toy store until the cartoon-like voices singing the same song repeatedly drove them to the edge, and stopping to talk with old acquaintances, Rachel and Liz would relax at a wrought iron table surrounded by trees and fountains, enjoying quiche, salad, and black bean soup in a bread bowl, while discussing which movie they wanted to see that night.

Liz saw very little of her old high school friends when she was home. Although at graduation many had tearfully promised to keep in touch forever, that hadn't happened. It seemed that most of her class had gone out of their way to get as far from home as possible, and only came back to town for brief visits. Even when home, everyone was busy and rarely had time to find out who was in town, much less get together. So, vacation time was family time, and Liz's parents relished their monopoly.

For the first few days, Liz let them spoil her all they wanted to. But by the end of the week she gently put her foot down and told her parents that she wanted some time to go out alone. They consented, and Liz was free for the morning. Wandering around the Galleria in a crowd was almost like being back at school, minus the backpack, the deadlines, being late for class, and eating on the run. OK, it *wasn't* like school, but there was something familiar in the air.

Above the noise of the crowd, a love song was echoing, dreamlike, off the ceiling. Liz recognized it as one that had always tugged at her heart, about finding that someone out there somewhere. It reawakened the sense of longing she had been trying to forget. She began to walk a little faster, as though picking up the pace would help her escape the feelings that were beginning to flood her senses.

Chapter Nine

Glancing from one window display to another, she began chattering to herself in her mind, as if to convince herself that she was fascinated by the merchandise.

Hey, I like that T-shirt. Ooo, nice sandals, wonder if they have them in my size. Cute purse to match. How much money have I got?

Then, she stopped abruptly. Directly in front of her was an exquisite wedding gown of satin trimmed with intricate lace and tiny pearl beads. The slender mannequin had long auburn curls and large, bashful green eyes that stared into hers. Liz stared back.

"You'd make a beautiful bride," a voice said from behind her. Liz froze. She knew that voice! She was afraid to turn around.

"You know, real beauty comes from within. No need to spend a fortune on satin and pearls." Liz looked at the reflection in the window and clapped her hand over her mouth to suppress a gasp. There behind her stood a thin, slightly twisted body leaning on a cane, his leg in a brace. He had a familiar face, though the eyes were hidden by the reflection off a pair of thick lenses. Trembling, she turned around.

"Do I know you?" she asked cautiously.

"Of course you do," he smiled.

"What are you doing here?"

He smiled. "Enjoying your company."

"But where have you *been*? I've been looking all over for you!" she cried, her eyes filling with tears.

"No need to look all over," he replied simply. "I'm always with you."

As the tears of joy spilled down her cheeks, Liz threw her arms around him, crying, "I thought I'd never see you again!" As she embraced him, he felt soft and warm, and the next thing she realized was that her face was buried not in J's shoulder, but her own tear-stained pillow.

Chapter Ten

Rachel was passing Liz's room when she heard a muffled cry of frustration. "NO-o-o-o-o!"

Concerned, she tapped on the door.

"Elizabeth? Are you all right?" Not waiting for an answer, she opened the door to find her daughter lying on the bed in tears. Liz quickly sat up and wiped her cheeks with her sleeve.

"Honey, what's wrong?" Rachel hurried over and put her arms around her daughter. "Don't you feel well?"

Liz pulled herself together and replied as casually as she could, "It's nothing, Mom, I just had a dream, that's all."

Rachel still seemed alarmed. "Oh, Elizabeth, you and your dreams! Darling, if you're having nightmares, maybe you should talk to Dr. Schneider again."

"Mom, I don't need a shrink," Liz replied testily.

"But maybe he could . . ."

"Mom, I'm *fine!*" she snapped. Then quickly regaining her composure, she added, "Really, I'm OK. It was just a dream, don't worry."

Rachel looked uncertain. "Well, all right, dear, if you say so." She got up hesitantly and began to leave. At the door she turned to

Liz and said, "We're going to church at eleven o'clock for the Palm Sunday service. Would you like to come?"

"Sure," said Liz cheerfully. She didn't really want to go, but she wanted to be sure her mother was convinced that she was all right, and staying in bed all morning was certainly not going to do that. Besides, it was impossible to get back into a dream; she had tried it before. *May as well, go*, she told herself.

But for a while she lingered in bed, staring listlessly. A tree in the yard cast a shadow on the ceiling, the same tree that had been outside her window since she was a small child. She had frequently lain awake at night, staring at the shadow cast by the streetlight outside. On a windless night the shadow had appeared in the perfect shape of an angel and it had made Liz feel safe and secure. She remembered nights when she had been sick with one of her frequent bouts of bronchitis or pneumonia. Even as the rest of the household had been asleep, as long as she could see her "angel" above her, she never felt alone. Now, however, the shadow was just a mass of nondescript blobs, as meaningless as her life seemed at the moment.

"Can't get back into childhood either, I suppose," she murmured.

Palm Sunday was sunny and glorious, and the white steeple of the church shone proudly against the blue sky. The jonquils scattered in front of the church waved invitingly in the warm breeze as the faithful flocked through the open doors. Inside, the pews were packed with upper-class churchgoers, many of them middle-aged with college-aged children home on break, most of whom were familiar to Liz. There were soft greetings as the Danfields came in. Women flawlessly dressed exchanged silent, exaggerated smiles, waves, and blown kisses across the sanctuary as the organ loudly played the prelude. Liz already knew how it would be after church: "Oh Rachie, Rachie, Rachie! This can't be little Elizabeth! Such a young lady now! So beautiful!" Yadda, yadda, yadda.

Liz stifled a yawn and looked at the massive stained-glass window over the altar. Unlike her angel-tree-shadow, this had not changed, and with the morning sun streaming through the jewel-

Chapter Ten

like panels, it was as dazzling as she had remembered it. She had always thought it to be the most interesting thing about church, although it seemed this morning that a fashion show of sorts was going on.

Ah, yes, Palm Sunday, she remembered. *The unveiling of the spring line.*

The organist finished the prelude and the service began with the traditional "Carol of the Palms." Liz smiled at the cherub-faced children who toddled in with their palm branches, and she suppressed a chuckle when a woman sitting on the aisle had to duck to dodge the frond waved by an over-zealous five-year-old, lest it knock off her Neiman-Marcus hat. The voices of the children were sweetly off key, the song familiar, the mood joyous and nostalgic. Liz was glad she had come.

After announcements, hymns, prayer, the Lord's Prayer, the offering, the doxology, all in predictable order, the minister, Carl A. Lambert, Doctor of Divinity, predictably stepped up to the pulpit to read the scripture, his flowing robe looking very impressive and official. His voice was impressive, too, no doubt from years of training.

Liz wished he would talk like a normal human being.

". . . and may the Lord bless to us the reading of His Word." And all the people said, "Amen."

As Dr. Lambert settled into his sermon, Liz settled into boredom mode. She had enjoyed the hymns—she had forgotten how uplifting they could be—and she decided to page through the hymnal to pass the time. As she reached for the book, Rachel began to say something to her about fidgeting in church, but apparently remembering in time that her daughter was, after all, twenty-one years old, she stopped herself. Instead, she sat stiffly, staring straight ahead, hoping none of her friends would notice Liz's faux pas.

Now, what hymn was it we just sang? Liz opened the book, but instead of seeing music, she saw two columns of print, and at the top of the page the one word, "Isaiah." *Oops, this isn't a hymnal, it's a Bible.*

69

Counselor

She was about to close it when her eyes spotted words that made her heart stop.

He had no beauty or majesty to attract us to him,
nothing in his appearance that we should desire him.

What was it about those words that struck a chord in her soul? An image of a bent body crossed her mind, and her heart began to beat faster. She read on.

He was despised and rejected by men,
a man of sorrows, and familiar with suffering.

She had a flashback of her dream in which her friend had experienced the pain of rejection as Amber had turned and coldly walked away.

Like one from whom men hide their faces,
he was despised, and we esteemed him not.

Now her heart was pounding. This was her dearest friend! She felt that once again she was sitting across the little table, confiding in him all of her hurts and disappointments.

Surely he has born our infirmities and carried our sorrows . . .*

Tears welled up in her eyes with the overwhelming feeling that at last she had found him.

* Isaiah 53:2b–4a (NIV)

Chapter Eleven

𝒟r. Lambert stood at the door as people lined up to shake his hand; he looked like a dignitary in a receiving line. Liz and her parents were last in line, largely due to George's socializing and parading his daughter around as though none of these people had ever had the privilege of meeting her before. At last they stepped up to the minister. Dr. Lambert gave Liz a hearty handshake and a broad smile that showed just enough teeth. *He must have studied theater,* Liz thought.

"I really enjoyed the service," she said, truthfully enough. Rachel seemed surprised when she added, "I have a question." George looked proud—his daughter, the intellectual!

"Well," Dr. Lambert replied with as much modesty as he could muster, "I can't guarantee I have the answer, but ask anyway."

Liz took a deep breath. "Well," she began, "there's a chapter in Isaiah —chapter 53—that talks about a tender root from dry ground or something. Then it describes a man who was unlovely and despised and rejected and familiar with suffering. Who was Isaiah writing about?"

Counselor

Dr. Lambert paused for effect. "It's funny you should ask about that particular chapter. It's one of my favorites." Seeing his knowing smile, Liz listened eagerly for his reply.

"Isaiah lived about the eighth century B.C. This passage was—"

"Dr. Lambert, I want you to meet Roger's family!" A woman who was vaguely familiar to Liz interrupted her inquiry. "This is John Wilson and his wife Shirley. We're *so* looking forward to your officiating at Roger and Amanda's wedding, and . . ."

As the woman took the minister's arm and babbled on, Liz shyly backed away, embarrassed that she may have taken more than her fair share of his time. Anyway, she had the answer she was looking for, though it was a disappointing one. The description she had read had been so profound, that of a person who knew suffering well, who loved deeply, sacrificially. She had begun to think that the J actually stood for . . . But that couldn't be. Not if Isaiah had written it eight hundred years before He was born. Liz sighed, frustrated that she seemed to have come so close to the answer, only to have the darkness close in on her again.

"Mom, do we have a Bible?" Liz asked when they got home.
"Um, I think there's one in the den."

Liz turned to go, and her mother's eyes followed her with concern. Why all this interest in the Bible all of a sudden? She hoped her daughter wasn't going off the deep end again.

Holy Bible. The words were embossed in ornate, gold letters on the black leather cover. The book squeaked when Liz opened it, and by the way some of the pages stuck together, it was apparent that it had had little use. She looked at the table of contents and noted that there were two main sections, Old Testament and New Testament. *Oh yeah, I remember now,* she thought, as visions of primary Sunday school flashed through her mind. *The Old is* B.C., *the New is* A.D.

Remembering Dr. Lambert's words, she looked in the Old Testament table of contents and found Isaiah. Turning to chapter 53, she began to read the whole chapter.

Chapter Eleven

Who has believed our message
>and to whom has the arm of the
>>Lord been revealed?

He grew up before him like a tender
>shoot,
>>and like a root out of dry ground.

He had no beauty or majesty to attract
>us to him,
>>nothing in his appearance that we
>>should desire him.

He was despised and rejected by men,
>a man of sorrows, and familiar with
>>suffering.

Like one from whom men hide their
>faces
>>he was despised, and we esteemed
>>him not.

Surely he took up our infirmities
>and carried our sorrows,

yet we considered him stricken by
>God,
>>smitten by him and afflicted.

But he was pierced for our
>transgressions,
>>he was crushed for our iniquities;

the punishment that brought us peace
>was upon him,
>>and by his wounds we are healed.*

Wow, Liz thought. *If this wasn't Old Testament, I could swear it was about* . . . Again she dismissed the thought. If only she could ask someone who knew. Then she half laughed at herself, as the obvious answer lay there in her lap. *Yeah, I suppose I could ask Him.*

Liz had often heard Sarah say that God answers prayer, but she had never taken it too seriously. She had always thought of prayer as asking for stuff, and if the person were good enough, and if the prayer had the right number of *"thees"* and *"thous"* and the person didn't ask for anything too big or too fun for himself, *maybe* it

Counselor

would happen—*if* it was God's will. She had always heard that clause as a type of divine loophole. Was it God's will for her to understand about J?

Liz had to think about it for a while. She wished she knew more about God. Sarah had talked frequently as if she knew Him personally, but Liz had always been preoccupied with the theater—preoccupied with herself, she now realized. But as she thought of Sarah, whose transparency had always contrasted with the social game-playing of other people she knew, she thought, if Sarah was a reflection of the God she served, He would want her to know the truth. Wouldn't He?

Wouldn't hurt to ask, she thought. She closed the door to the den. She curled up on the love seat with the Bible and stared for a minute at the gold lettering, as though it might give her some guidance. Finally she started to speak, softly and hesitantly.

"God . . . um, Almighty God. I . . . I don't know You very well. I guess that's my fault, huh? I guess You know all about me. I dream a lot, I cry too easily, I try too hard . . . Anyway, I hope You're listening.

"I think You must care about me, because Sarah always acted like she cared, and she knows You like a friend, and . . ." *This is getting nowhere*, Liz thought. But she decided to keep trying.

"Um, I was hoping You could help me . . . if You don't mind. I need to understand something. Who was Isaiah talking about, and what does he have to do with the man in my dream? Is J a real person? If not, why do I keep dreaming about him? Can You . . . I mean *would* You tell me who he is? I mean, if You talk to people like me. I don't want to be too demanding . . . I just need to know what to do. If he's not real, please help me to stop thinking about him, so I can get on with my life." Liz felt a stabbing pain in her heart. If remembering J was painful, the thought of forgetting him was worse. A tear fell onto her hand as she added,

"But could I . . . I mean, if it's OK with You . . . could I see him just once more . . ."—she swallowed hard—". . . so I can tell him goodbye?"

Chapter Eleven

George wandered into the kitchen where the "oldies" station was playing "You Needed Me," and his face softened with the warmth of a good memory. Rachel was standing at the sink washing vegetables; he gave her a playful squeeze.

"Hey, lady," he whispered. "They're playing our song." But Rachel's thoughts were elsewhere.

"Liz has been in the den an awfully long time." Her voice sounded concerned. "You'd think she'd get enough reading at school."

George sighed and went to check on his daughter. He tapped lightly on the door to the den. Then, hearing no response, he quietly opened it. Liz was curled up on the love seat, sound asleep, her arms wrapped around the Bible. George smiled at the memory of a little girl hugging her favorite toy. He covered her with the white afghan, kissed the top of her head, and tiptoed back out.

Liz sat under the familiar tree on the quad, sunshine splashing gold through her hair. Her guitar rested in her lap, surrounded by the folds of her long, white dress. As her fingers moved nimbly across the strings, diamonds sparkled on her left hand, and tiny pearls shimmered in the exquisite lace of her sleeves. She sang a song about a friend who had dried her tears, who had bought back the soul she had sold, who had given her clarity and dignity, and who had somehow needed her, too.

Her voice had never been so strong or confident, and her smile was radiant. She had been given the strength to live, the courage to face life, and somehow a glimpse of eternity as well.

She stopped when she saw another shadow beside hers, that of a slender form, slightly twisted. She turned quickly to see him, and when their eyes met, he straightened a little and smiled at her. His hair hung free, the thick glasses were gone, and his eyes were like shining stars.

"You came!" she cried, her joy mingled with dread. "Can you stay . . . or do you have to leave?"

He gave her that same warm smile and replied, "Liz, I told you, I am always with you. Are you ready to be my bride?"

Counselor

Liz knew this was another dream, but she also knew that something about it was very real. Perhaps the only way to find out was to follow her heart.

"Yes, I'm ready," she said, rising to her feet. A warm wind blew through the long auburn curls, and white satin fluttered around her feet.

"Come," he invited. "Be one with me forever."

He now straightened completely. To Liz's surprise, as he reached for her his fingers uncurled. She had never really seen his hands open before, but now as she looked at them for the first time, she was thunderstruck.

In the center of each one there was a gaping wound.

* Isaiah 53 (NIV)

Chapter Twelve

So, now she knew without a doubt what "J" stood for. She hardly dared to speak His name—the name Sarah loved, the name that was frequently abused at the university, a name Liz had for some reason been uncomfortable speaking. Now suddenly it seemed to her the most beautiful name in the world.

She sat there in the study, feeling the soft leather of the easy chair around her like big, strong arms. She stared at the oak shelves surrounding her, the clusters of hardbound books, separated by frames containing photographs of a smiling couple and two little girls. As Liz gazed at the familiar pictures, scenes from her childhood passed through her mind like the memory of a dream gradually coming into focus.

As a small child in Sunday school Liz had seen pictures of Jesus, and she now remembered what a warm feeling they had given her. He was always surrounded by children—a chubby baby on His lap, a little girl offering Him flowers. Liz always wondered what it would have felt like to be one of them. Would Jesus have spoken to her? Would He have looked into her eyes? Would He have let her hug Him?

When she had first received her very own Bible in the fourth grade, Liz had eagerly begun reading it, knowing it was a very special book. She had read all the familiar stories in Genesis and Exodus, until, getting bogged down in Leviticus with the ancient Jewish laws that had seemed so confusing and impossible and irrelevant, she had set the Bible aside in favor of Nancy Drew.

With the teenage years and her growing sense of insignificance had come a sense that God was distant and uninvolved. Occasionally, in a crisis, she had impulsively asked for His help, but at the same time had felt she might as well have been talking to someone on Mars. Youth group at church had not been a time of spiritual growth, but rather one more source of entertainment. Liz's memories of the group consisted mainly of bowling or skating with the other teens in the church, and since Liz had liked neither bowling nor skating, she had gradually dropped out. If anyone had ever invited her to rejoin the group, she might have considered it, but no one had.

Later, there had been that search for a soul-mate, and the painful discovery that not all boys were interested in what she thought, that some would lie to get what they wanted, and that if they didn't get what they wanted they were quite capable of lying and saying that they had. Liz had time and again become disillusioned about life, about friendship, about trust.

Could it really be that Jesus had been there all that time? Could He have been listening to her heart, even though the words were unspoken? Had He understood and cared? Or was she just a wishful thinker, dreaming dreams?

Chapter Thirteen

The Danfields lived in a quiet neighborhood with stately homes, hundred-year-old trees, and magnificently landscaped yards. In this pleasant setting, the family frequently enjoyed leisurely walks together.

Thursday evening George and Liz had finally coaxed Rachel out of the kitchen to make the most of the fresh air and what was left of the daylight, and to stretch their legs after Rachel's superb dinner. As they strolled the quiet street, Liz was thinking that April was the most beautiful time of year in St. Louis. The spring rains had turned the lawns emerald green and brought out the jonquils, hyacinths, and crocuses. Pink and white dogwoods adorned the landscape, along with the deeper pink redbud trees, and the delicate yellow-green leaves just beginning to emerge on the larger trees that towered over them.

In a well-manicured yard an elderly man in grass-stained jeans and flannel shirt was spreading mulch around a white dogwood tree. George, who was no respecter of persons when it came to talking and had never been known to pass anyone without speaking, greeted the man. Rachel began to say something but stopped short and merely sighed; they might be here a while.

"Great job you do on this yard." George complimented the man sincerely. The man smiled awkwardly.

"George Danfield," George said, extending his hand. The man rubbed his dirt-encrusted hand on his pants and shyly shook hands with him.

"Yep, we've had a good spring," he responded modestly. "I do love comin' here—gettin' my hands in the dirt again." He grinned, exposing a gap in his crooked teeth, and well-embedded smile lines around his eyes deepened.

"Well, you do have the gift," said Rachel, taking a step and hoping her husband would come along. No such luck. Liz suppressed a smile.

"This is a dogwood, isn't it?" said George. "I love these."

"So do I," said the yardman with a knowing smile. "'The Easter trees,' I like to call 'em." His expression invited the question.

"Why?" asked Liz. Rachel bit her tongue.

"Well," began the man, stepping up to the tree and gently taking one of the branches in his leathery hand, "you see the way the blossoms are shaped?" Liz and George stepped closer and looked; each blossom had four petals, two that were long and two shorter. "They're shaped like a cross. The story goes that this is the tree that was used to crucify Jesus."

"Isn't it kind of small?" asked Liz, suspecting that there was more to the story.

"It is *now*," the man stated with an air of authority. "Y'see, the tree felt so bad 'bout being used that way that the Lord felt sorry for it. So, He made it all small and twisted, so nobody'd use it like that again."

"What a cool story!" said Liz, noticing for the first time how twisted the tree's little trunk was.

"And look here," said the man, whose face was beaming now. He pointed to one of the white blossoms with a gnarled finger. "See the nail marks? And the blood stains?" Liz looked at the familiar crimped, darkened edges of the petals, seeing them in a new light.

"Wow," she breathed.

Chapter Thirteen

"Well, I'll be," murmured George. "How about that?"

Liz was silent for a moment, gazing at the blossoms in awe. *Even in nature, the story is told!*

None of them had noticed dark storm clouds moving in, but suddenly, almost simultaneously, each of them felt a raindrop.

"We'd better pick up the pace," said Rachel. "There's a storm moving in." The Danfields said goodbye to the yardman, who was beginning to gather up his tools, and started walking briskly toward home. As the raindrops fell more rapidly, the family trotted more swiftly. By the time they had reached their driveway they were running. Rachel shrieked and covered her hair as George took her arm to keep her from slipping in the puddles. The rain was coming down in sheets by the time the three burst through the door, breathless, drenched, and laughing.

"Well, you two," panted Rachel, shaking the water from her auburn curls, "any more great ideas?"

An hour later, the three of them were dry and relaxing in the living room. Thunder still rumbled outside and raindrops drummed on the windows. An occasional flash of lightning caused the lights to flicker. Otherwise, it was a typical evening at home. George sat in the recliner, his reading glasses perched on his nose, to read the newspaper and watch the television simultaneously. Liz lay on the floor in front of the TV, dutifully stretching in preparation for some of her theater exercises. Rachel had just come in from going over the kitchen one last time. She nervously moved a tiered table of fragile knickknacks out of the way of Liz's extended toes before picking up one of the fashion magazines on the coffee table. Liz had discovered part two of a miniseries about the life of Christ, which at this point captured her attention. There was an all-star cast, yet the man portraying Jesus was relatively unknown. The director must have worked hard to achieve that ethereal look, for although this man was strikingly handsome, he always seemed to have his head in another world. Something about him bothered Liz, but for a while she couldn't put her finger on it. Finally she came to realize what it was.

81

Counselor

"I don't think He was really like that," Liz suddenly remarked during one scene. She had finished her exercises and was seated on the floor doing her "cooling down" stretches.

Rachel looked up from her magazine. "Don't think who was like what?" she asked.

"I don't think Jesus was all head-in-the-clouds like that. I think He's more . . . I mean, I think He was more . . . down-to-earth."

"Down-to-earth? Honey, He was the Lord," George said delicately.

"I know, but He was human, too. I mean, wasn't that the point? He became one of us, right? And how do they know He was that good-looking? Is there anything in the Bible that says He was gorgeous?"

"Well, as your father said, He *was* the *Lord*." Rachel seemed uncomfortable with this conversation.

"I don't suppose there's anything in the Bible that says He was attractive," said George. "But, since He had so many followers, I guess the folks in Hollywood assumed He must've had charisma."

"Maybe," Liz said thoughtfully. "But look who followed Him. They were people like fishermen—the poor, the sick, the sinners. The 'huddled masses.' He didn't have many followers who were rich or famous, did He?"

George lowered his newspaper. "Y'know, I'm not sure. I'm afraid I'm not much of a Bible scholar," he added sheepishly. Just then the cameras focused on a group of the religious elite of the day, who were scowling jealously at the handsome Carpenter who was attracting so much attention.

"The people in power hated Him, didn't they?" Liz was thinking out loud. "The people who thrived on appearances. Jesus kind of attacked their showiness, didn't He?"

"Yes, I guess He did, come to think of it," said George. "Called them hypocrites." Liz turned to him.

"You know what I think, Dad? I think He was more like the common people. No big deal to look at, but it was what He said, and *how* He said it. They knew He loved them and cared about them. They weren't getting that from their religious leaders. Those

Chapter Thirteen

guys were too busy showing off and judging everyone." As Liz was being carried along by this train of thought, it was as though she could see J's face as He listened, His eyes coaching her along in her discovery.

"They loved to tell everybody what to do, but Jesus could *show* them the way, not just *tell* them. He could be their Friend *and* their Healer *and* their Teacher *and* their . . . Counselor! Dad, He's *wonderful!*"

George looked both curious and amused at her enthusiasm. Wanting to share the moment, he added, "That's right—'Wonderful Counselor!' Doesn't the Bible say that somewhere, honey?" He looked at Rachel, who was becoming more uncomfortable with the discussion by the minute.

"Somewhere, yes," she mumbled, turning the page of her magazine. "Elizabeth, you talk like you know Him personally."

Liz looked pensive, as she murmured, "Maybe I do."

George removed his glasses and put them in their case. Folding the paper, he stretched and yawned. "Well, honey, much as I'm enjoying this discussion, I think I'd better head for the barn before I turn into a pumpkin." Laying the paper down, he stepped over to his daughter and kissed the top of her head.

"'Night, Dad," said Liz, giving him a quick smile and returning her attention to the program.

It wasn't long before Rachel closed her magazine and sighed. "Goodness, I'm tired too, all of a sudden. Busy day." Liz knew that most of that busy day had been spent in the kitchen, and although Rachel loved to cook, she did have a tendency to get carried away, even when cooking just for her not-quite-gourmet family.

"*Great* dinner, Mom," said Liz. "I *love* your coq au vin." Rachel seemed pleased.

"Thank you, darling," she said, kissing her. "Can you make sure the lights are all off before you come up?"

"Sure, Mom. G'night."

"Goodnight. See you in the morning."

Liz's eyes became riveted to the scenes that followed: the arrest of Jesus, the disciples' desertion, the trial, Peter's denial and remorse at the cock's crowing, the flogging of Jesus. Now more vulnerable, He looked more like the J that she knew. Liz winced at every blow of the whip, the tears welling up in her eyes. When the flogging was over, her Friend hung limp, his hair soaked with blood and sweat. As the soldiers mocked and roared with laughter, she realized just how much He did understand rejection—far better than she did.

As she witnessed Christ's agony on the cross—something that had always been to her an example of "man's inhumanity to man"—she sensed something new and wonderful. Not so much the horror of torture and death, but the wonder and magnitude of the love that allowed Him to go through it to redeem humanity—to redeem *her*.

"Oh, Jesus," she whispered, "You really do love me, don't You?"

The thought gave her such unexpected peace that she must have fallen asleep at that moment, or perhaps experienced some kind of vision, for invading her mind was a tangled montage of scenes, memories, and fantasies that seemed at first to be unrelated.

Jesus was still being flogged. Liz could see at a disturbingly close range the cuts opening up His back, the blood spurting from each wound. She saw a tiny girl with auburn curls kneeling by her bed and asking Jesus to be her Savior. She saw a couple in the Student Union talking intimately over coffee. She saw the auburn-haired girl, a little older, setting aside her Bible and picking up a paper-back novel. She saw another cut of the whip, more blood, and Amber turning and walking away.

A group of grade-school girls were giggling and making fun of an overweight classmate with thick glasses. One of them, a shy-looking girl with auburn curls laughed less heartily than the others, but when another girl looked at her and said, "Right, Liz?" the girl attempted a "cool" smirk and, with forced nastiness, sneered "Yeah! Right!" She remembered with shame that that instance of betrayal had not won her any status among the fourth grade elite, but had only caused her remorse. Again the whip cracked; again blood was shed.

Chapter Thirteen

A teenager with bashful green eyes watched her mother leave the kitchen. She then hurriedly took her plate and dumped her dinner down the garbage disposal. Instantly, Liz saw a bony figure standing on a bathroom scale that registered ninety pounds. She heard another crack of the whip and saw a handicapped student stumble painfully on a lame leg.

Liz saw flashbacks of every attempt she had made to succeed in the theater, including every compromise, every profanity that was "part of the script," every time she had ignored the still, small voice within in favor of courting the world. The images were now flashing by to the rhythm of a pounding hammer. Finally, the image came of a thin body, twisted in agony, nailed to a cross. She couldn't bear the sight. Cringing, she looked down and saw that in her hand was a heavy mallet. Horrified, she dropped it, buried her face in her hands, and cried, "Forgive me, Jesus! I didn't know . . . !" Looking up, she saw a huge tree with two limbs extended outward, quickly becoming the crossbars of a crucifix, then withering into a twisted, humiliated little shrub that the next moment burst into a multitude of white blossoms.

A sudden loud clap of thunder woke her with a start just in time to hear the parting words of Jesus to His followers. They were familiar words, now indescribably precious, since they had twice been spoken directly to her.

"I am with you always."

Again she sensed His forgiveness, and again the thought of such an incredible love flooded her with peace.

With her always—in spite of everything.

What a Friend.

Chapter Fourteen

"Everett!" a little girl scolded her baby brother. The tot had helped himself to a chocolate marshmallow egg from a crystal candy dish, then predictably wiped his chubby hands on his brand new Easter suit; his mother, apparently a glutton for punishment, had chosen white. The big sister grabbed the chocolate-smeared hands amid his wails of protest, and wiped them clean with a napkin.

"Come on!" she cried with exaggerated excitement. "Let's go find some eggs!" She thus changed his tears to squeals of enthusiasm and led him away from the patio to the lush, green lawn of the country club. There, well-dressed children scampered about while parents snapped pictures and videotaped. With their pastel Easter outfits, the children looked like spring flowers blowing in the wind. As tiny hands reached under bushes and into clumps of grass, baskets tipped and the hard-boiled treasures rolled out almost as often as they were collected.

Liz smiled, reminiscing, as she and her parents passed them on their way to the dining room. But it was more than cute toddlers and happy memories that made her face glow with such contentment that morning. She was still feeling the effects of the celebration earlier at church, and thinking that Easter had never been so glorious. As the congregation had sung the traditional Easter hymn, "Christ the Lord is Ris'n Today," the organ booming out the notes triumphantly, it had been as though she were hearing it—*really* hearing it—for the first time.

She had felt as though she could sing it all day; indeed, it was still ringing in her mind and heart. The classic words had suddenly made sense to her, because she was understanding for the first time how much Jesus really loved humanity—how much He loved *her*. It would take the rest of her life to understand it completely, but she was certain it would be a joyous process. Now it seemed the sun had never shone so brightly, the grass had never been so green, the hyacinth so fragrant.

"'Mornin', Mr. Danfield!" came the jovial voice of the doorman, as George and his family were given the red-carpet treatment.

"Morning, Irving. And a happy Easter to you!" came George's jovial reply.

"Thank you, sir! Same to you!"

They stepped into a spacious dining room that was aglow with spring colors and filled with the smells of brunch. The clinking of fine china and murmur of soft, civilized voices contrasted with the bustle of busy waiters and the occasional whine of a restless child. The moment they walked in George spotted friends—a group of physicians sharing a story over martinis. Rachel sighed as her husband immediately began making his way over to say hello; she knew he had been waiting for the opportunity to tell them his latest joke.

"Good morning, Mrs. Danfield. Table for three?" asked the hostess uncertainly.

"Uh, sure," said Rachel. "I'm sure he'll find us." George could be heard enjoying the spotlight as he told his story. "A doctor, a nurse, and an HMO provider all died and went to the Pearly Gates . . ."

The hostess seated the ladies and asked if they'd like menus. Rachel and Liz declined in favor of the special Easter brunch. The immense buffet lined an entire wall, behind which one could look

Chapter Fourteen

out through the picture windows onto the green fairway, where one lone golf fanatic was already teeing off.

"So," George's good-humored voice could be heard, "St. Peter says to the HMO provider, 'OK, you can come in, too. But you can only stay three days.'" As the doctors chuckled heartily, George waved good-bye and came to rejoin his family. "Leave 'em laughin'" was George's motto.

The socializing continued as the family went through the buffet line. Liz dutifully said hello and shook hands as Rachel prompted, "You remember the Rothchilds, don't you, dear? And the Stevenses?" During the course of the morning, Liz greeted a bank president, three lawyers, a judge, two doctors, and a senator. But though she smiled and made the perfunctory small talk, something in her was yearning to get away, to just be alone . . . with Him.

"Liz?" her mother's voice snapped her out of her reverie, and she realized a waiter was offering her more coffee.

"Oh . . . uh, thank you," she responded absently. A moment later, she felt her father take her hand and place something in it.

A penny. She smiled. As long as she could remember, this had been her father's way of saying, "Penny for your thoughts." Even as a little girl, she had known that she had to tell him what she had been thinking or give him a refund.

"How about it, Kiddo?" he teased with a twinkle in his eye. "Your mind is miles away. In paradise by the look of it." He paused as an idea struck him. "You aren't in love, are you?"

"George!" scolded Rachel. "Must you be so blunt?" She shook her head apologetically to her daughter. But, by the subtle way she was smiling, Liz could tell that her mother, too, would want to hear all about a budding romance.

Liz hesitated, wondering how to explain what was happening to her. She wasn't sure she knew herself. The way her parents obsessed over her mental stability, she certainly didn't want them to think she was going off the religious deep end. Besides, this wasn't religion, it was something so much better.

No, not "something." Some*one*.

"I . . . just . . . I love spring," she stammered, truthfully enough, gazing at the arrangement of jonquils, tulips, and hyacinths on the table. "It's been such a long winter, I'm glad it's over."

George and Rachel seemed to accept that explanation, and Liz got to keep the penny.

Seeing Liz staring at the centerpiece, her mother exclaimed. "Aren't these gorgeous! I've never seen the flowers more beautiful than they are this year. Did you see the jonquils and narcissus on the hill in front of the church? Why don't we all go for a walk when we get home!"

George glanced at his plate, laden with French toast, eggs, and sausage. "If I can still move." He laughed.

It wasn't Liz's plate but her heart that was overflowing, where the triumphant resurrection music played on.

Chapter Fifteen

Liz had mixed emotions about returning to school. Spring break had been both refreshing and exciting, but the refreshing part was starting to get old, and even the excitement of the discoveries she had made stirred up in her a restlessness to see where it all was leading. Somehow she felt that Sarah and her friends had the answers—and they were back at school.

Of course, there was another reason to get back to school, and whenever the thought of the spring musical crossed her mind, the butterflies in her stomach gave an ecstatic flutter. With costume fittings and rehearsals beginning to take place on the actual stage, in front of some actual scenery, the reality was starting to hit home. This was not just another scene for acting class. This was the real thing. One moment Liz would be thinking, "I can't wait!" and the next she'd be gripped with anxiety as she gazed out at all the empty seats. What if she blew it, in front of all those people?

Of course, there were still classes to attend, papers to write. The current assignment for English Lit was sheer nuisance. *Why do actors have to write papers, anyway?* she griped. Of course, she knew that a BFA required courses in a variety of subjects, and the university was doing her a favor by letting her make up the subjects she had been unable to finish the semester she'd had pneumonia. Still, having the irrelevant assignment hang over her head was like having to carry an umbrella in a swimming pool.

"OK," she said to herself in her no-nonsense voice as she sat at the kitchen table and wrote in the margin of her notebook. "This isn't so bad. I can get it all done tomorrow night, since there's no rehearsal. Read the rest of the book." She flipped through the pages. "A hundred pages to go—about two hours of reading, knowing me. Do that from six to eight. I'll just grab dinner right after class. The paper I can write in about an hour and a half. So, that's nine-thirty. I can type it in about an hour—better make that an hour and a half. OK, nine-thirty to eleven. Hey! Piece of cake!" She tried to feel satisfied, and reassured, but she sighed in disgust. Writing an English paper was not her favorite way to spend an evening. *Oh well, gotta graduate.*

The phone was a welcome interruption to this dreary subject, and Liz perked up to hear Sarah's voice on the line.

"Hey, Liz! I got your message. What's up?"

"Sarah! Yeah, I called because I . . ." How to sum it all up? "You know that thing you go to with your religious—" oops! Sarah *hated* to be called religious "—your Christian friends?"

"You mean Intervarsity?"

"Intervarsity! That's it. Well, I'd kinda like to come to one of them."

"Great! We'd love to have you!" Sarah sounded excited. "In fact, there's a meeting tomorrow night!"

Tomorrow night!

"Oh, shoot, I have to write a paper tomorrow night."

"Oh," Sarah sounded deflated. "Can't you write it tonight?"

"No, I've got rehearsal tonight."

"After rehearsal?"

"I wish. Rehearsals are starting to go really late, I'm usually exhausted when I get back."

"Oh, shoot." Sarah sounded even more let down than Liz.

Chapter Fifteen

"Maybe I can make the next one." Liz tried to sound optimistic. *Stupid paper!* she thought.

"I hope so, but there won't be that many more." Was Sarah thinking what Liz was thinking? Liz remembered having said "Maybe next time" before, but she'd never managed to get around to it.

"I really do want to go this time, Sarah. I have reasons. There's so much I want to talk to you about! Maybe you could pray that this dumb assignment would just go away."

"I will," said Sarah with a chuckle. "Well, let's get together *sometime*. Now you've got me curious! When's your next free evening?"

"I have no idea, maybe after the musical."

Sarah sighed. "The pressures of stardom, huh?"

"Yeah. Hey, keep in touch, OK?"

"Sure will. I'll be prayin' for ya."

Liz smiled. "Thanks, Sarah. I *mean* it. Well, I gotta run, or I'll be late for rehearsal. Talk to ya soon?"

"Yeah, definitely."

Liz reluctantly hung up the phone.

Oh, J . . . I mean Jesus, she prayed silently, *I know Sarah's invited me to that thing so many times before when I wasn't interested. Now I finally want to go, and . . .* she didn't know how to finish, and merely sighed with frustration as she headed out the door for rehearsal.

The English professor looked pale and tired as she entered the classroom. Instead of the usual booming voice greeting the class and getting right down to business, there was silence. Twenty-two freshmen and one senior sat in quiet anticipation, exchanging glances that said, *what's up?* The only sound in the room was the clacking of the woman's heels as she walked over to the board and wrote

1. *Due to my laryngitis, class is canceled today.*
2. *I don't have your last batch of papers graded yet.*
3. *The essay assignment is canceled. Just finish the book. Discussion on Monday.*

The freshmen murmured "Awri-i-ight!" and "Yessss!" under their breath, as the prof, seemingly too tired or sick to care, exited. The students waited a respectable few minutes before bursting through the door to enjoy their unexpected freedom until their next class.

Liz lingered a moment longer, staring at the message on the board. *Like handwriting from heaven*, she thought. She found herself grinning as she felt the privilege of being in on a secret joke. Sarah had been praying, and Liz would be at Intervarsity that night.

Chapter Sixteen

"I'm *so* glad you could come tonight!" Sarah bubbled.

"I know," Liz replied, grinning at her friend's enthusiasm. "You're the one that prayed me out of that assignment. I should have caught onto this prayer stuff my freshman year!" Both girls chuckled.

"So, all you have to do now is finish reading the book?"

"Not even that. When English got canceled, I did it then. Finished it before my next class. It's *done*," she announced with satisfaction.

"Wow, praise God." Sarah looked very satisfied, too.

Liz was surprised at the number of students packed into the lecture room at the Natural History Building. She wondered how many other classes and assignments had been canceled to get them all there.

"Are there always this many people?" she asked.

"Usually, yeah. Actually, Intervarsity has grown so big, there are four groups now."

"Four? You're kidding!"

Liz had somehow expected a few churchy-looking people sitting in pews with hymnals in their hands and solemn looks on their faces, but this bore no resemblance to church. Some students with electric guitars were in front, tuning up, and she was surprised to see Sean O'Brien from the theater department talking with one of them. He glanced up and seemed surprised to see her, too. His freckled face broke into a grin, and he greeted her with a silent wink and a "thumbs up."

Or perhaps the wink was for Sarah. They had the look of co-conspirators.

The students who filled the seats were hardly dressed for church. Jeans and T-shirts were the norm, and Liz was glad Sarah had talked her out of wearing a dress. The chatter seemed excited and casual. Liz had somehow expected that these people would be a little weird. She didn't know why; Sarah wasn't all that strange, except for her unusual level of enthusiasm.

Something else was different from church at home, although at first Liz could not put her finger on it. Then she realized what it was. While she was used to thinking of church as filled with white, upper-class members, this fellowship was white, African American, Hispanic, Oriental—in a word, humanity. The only commonalities here were in their age and their smiles.

The music started and it bore little resemblance to the church music at home. *Drums?* The students stood up as if on cue and started clapping and singing. Liz was at first afraid she'd stick out like a sore thumb because she didn't recognize the songs. But as she watched the musicians, she saw that the words were projected onto the wall behind them.

Wow. No hymnals. As she joined the others in clapping, she observed that having the lyrics up front left one's hands free for things other than holding a book. *Very practical*, she thought.

And fun! She had never had a thought containing the words "church" and "fun" at the same time. She had a feeling this might be a night of new ideas.

The words to the songs the students sang were not what she had expected either. Though she had always enjoyed the hymns at church, they often contained language from another time and place, and she had somehow felt that she was on the outside listening to

Chapter Sixteen

music from someone else's generation, a generation that didn't include children of divorce, computer junkies, or kids with spiked hair, baggy jeans, and skateboards. The words to these upbeat songs were as contemporary as the morning paper, yet the message was the same. They spoke of a God who was still alive and as concerned with this generation as He had been with any other. And judging from the expressions on the faces around her, Liz was beginning to think He could be a God Who liked to see His children happy.

Liz felt a chill. Whatever this was, it was wonderful. She never wanted it to stop.

As one song led into another the tempo slowed and the clapping stopped. Some of the students raised their hands, as if reaching heavenward for God. It wasn't long before Liz realized that to these students this wasn't just another activity to fill their time.

They sang that God was the very air they breathed, His Word their daily sustenance; they sang that they longed for Him, were even "desperate" for Him. How could it be that these students who seemed so in tune with God were singing the words that expressed exactly the hunger she felt? She sensed that what they were singing about was what she had been longing for; yet she didn't know how to reach it from where she was.

Although Liz tried not to show the emotions that were welling up in her, the tears were coming, and she knew she wouldn't be able to stop them; she wasn't sure she wanted to stop them. She raised her hands with the others, timidly at first, but it felt good to reach out for that something, or that Someone. She knew she was lost without Him. She wanted to know Him—to *really* know Him, and to really and truly worship Him. She had always thought of worship in terms of dry ritual, but this was so much more. The realization lit up her very soul—worship is what she was created to do! No wonder she had felt that desperation—that craving for something she knew she needed but hadn't been able to identify until now.

As the students continued singing, the craving was being satisfied, yet there was an ever-present hunger for more. The title of the song was "Shout to the Lord," but no one was shouting. It was more of a love song, and the description of Jesus sounded so much like J—the comfort and shelter He provided from life's storms, and the desire to worship Him with everything that was in her, to her dying breath. *Such passionate words.* Yet she meant every one. She felt a wave of joy come over her, as she sang wholeheartedly.

The theater was the farthest thing from her mind as the students sang in adoration, until the next event unexpectedly brought the two worlds together.

Two students, one of them Sean, acted out a scene, a short sketch about a young man's trying to have his "quiet time." Every time Sean said "OK, I'm going to read my Bible and pray!" the phone would ring, or there would be a knock at the door. And, every time there was a distraction, the other student, playing the part of the devil, would jump onto the young man's back and wrap his arms around his victim's neck. Each time, Sean would shake him off, but each time it became more and more difficult.

Finally, Sean shook him off for the last time, faced him, and said, "Satan, in the name of Jesus, you get out of here! You're not going to keep me from spending time with God!" As he picked up the devil and literally threw him off the stage, the audience cheered wildly, and Liz found herself applauding with them. It wasn't so much for the performers, though Liz was impressed with the authority with which Sean commanded the devil to leave, but for the victory that had been portrayed. It was like being at a sporting event and seeing someone score the winning point. There was such a sense of triumph.

But for what? The guy *gets to* read his Bible and pray. Liz remembered how important this habit had been to Sarah, but she had always thought it looked like a chore. Sarah would smile mischievously and say, "Don't knock it 'til you've tried it."

I suppose someone might think that spending time with a handicapped person looked like a chore, too. A good deed, maybe, but not very exciting.

The thought came unexpectedly, and she remembered how, in her dreams, seeing J was like an oasis in the desert, certainly not

Chapter Sixteen

what it might have appeared to be to an outsider. Maybe this "quiet time" thing was the same way.

The students quieted down as the speaker was introduced. His jeans and U of I sweat shirt couldn't hide the fact that he was a bit older than the students. They soon learned that he was an alumnus of the university. Although he bore little resemblance to Dr. Lambert, Liz wondered if this would be the boring part.

But the speaker's opening question caught her attention.

"Did you know that Christianity isn't a religion?"

What?

She noticed that many of the students were smiling knowingly, some nodding in agreement. After a brief pause, the speaker continued.

"Many people make the mistake of thinking Christianity is just one of many religions, but it's much more than that.

"Think about it. When someone says the word 'religion,' what do you think of? Stained glass windows, candles, solemn rituals? Prayers you've recited a thousand times? Wishing you were somewhere else, doing something else . . . *anything* else?" He paused, and a low murmur passed through the group.

"Too many of us were raised on religion—the duty, the ritual, the meaningless repetition. 'Sit up straight! Don't fidget!' And whatever you do, *don't laugh!*" A chuckle was heard in the back. The speaker scowled in mock disapproval.

"Are you having *fun* back there?

"But here's the best-kept secret of Christianity: It's a *relationship*. Now, what do you think of when you think of a relationship? A brother or sister, a parent, a friend, a close buddy, a lover?" He grinned. "Now it's getting more interesting, right?

"Did you know that Jesus wants to be with you, to talk to you, to counsel you, to bless you, to comfort you, to strengthen you, to laugh and cry with you—to just *love* you? And you don't have to have the books of the Bible memorized, or say the 'Our Father' or 'Hail Mary' or anything else. Just come to Him and say 'Jesus?' and you'll find He's already there. He wants to be your best friend, your confidant—He's a great listener—your 'Wonderful Counselor.'"

Liz was hanging on every word.

"He wants a relationship with you because He knows that the closer you are to Him, the more He can bless you, the more He can use you to bless others. The more you pray, the more He can *answer* your prayers and draw you closer to Him, so He can bless you even *more*.

"That's why the devil is so dead set against your having that quiet time, and he'll use every excuse in the book to keep you from it. Then, when it's been a while, and you feel that distance between you and Jesus, he'll discourage you with, 'You can't go to God *now*! Look how long it's been! Look what you've done!' etc. He's made it his job to separate you from God. It's *your* job to *resist* him, like our brother here did in the skit." He smiled at the two actors.

"You do have the authority to do it, did you know that? In Luke 10:19, Jesus said to His followers . . ." He opened his Bible and pages could be heard rustling throughout the auditorium. He read, "'I have given you authority to trample on snakes and scorpions, and to overcome all the power of the enemy; nothing will harm you.'"*

Liz felt a chill when he said the word "authority," though she didn't know why.

"So don't let him do it. Don't let Satan rob you of your most precious treasure—your relationship with the Lord. Listen to what else Jesus says." He turned the pages of his Bible and again read, "'The thief comes only to steal and kill and destroy; I have come that they might have life, and have it to the full.'**

"That's the life Jesus wants you to have with Him—*abundant life!*"

As the man went on, Liz began to realize two things. One was that she, like many others, had been deceived into thinking that Christianity was a tedious, unfulfilling religion. And the other was that, in spite of this attitude, she had, in a sense, already been experiencing this "quiet time" with Jesus. As she had been pouring out her heart to J, she had unknowingly been experiencing a taste of that abundant life this man was talking about. She had

Chapter Sixteen

missed spending these times with J so much. And now, with a thrill, she was beginning to think maybe she could still have them!

* *Luke 10:19 (NIV)*
** *John 10:10 (NIV)*

Chapter Seventeen

"So, Sarah," said Sean, "did you decide to take that job at Carle?"

Liz was seated at a table in a place called Delights with Sarah, Sean, and the other actor from the skit, whose name was Michael Tucker. She had overcome her anorexic tendencies and ordered a sundae with them, mainly to continue enjoying their fellowship.

"I haven't decided for sure. I'm still praying about it," Sarah replied. Then with a slight smile she added, "but it's looking like I probably will."

"They offered you a job at the hospital?" Liz asked, surprised that Sarah hadn't mentioned it.

"Yep, full time. I guess they liked my volunteer work."

"Well, that's no surprise."

Liz learned a number of things about her friends that night. She found out that Sean belonged to a rapidly growing church in the Chicago area and had already been offered a position as a youth pastor. The church's youth department was experiencing a veritable population explosion, and the pastoral staff was very interested in having Sean start a drama ministry. He had prayed about it and felt that this was what God was calling him to do.

Michael, an education major, had a "calling" to be a junior high science teacher. He was in the process of applying to public, private, and Christian schools, and was praying about where the Lord could use him most effectively. He seemed confident that God would show him.

Seems like everybody knows what they're doing except me, Liz thought. One thing the others all had in common was prayer. But how did they do it? Was there some secret formula?

"When you talk to God, is it just like you're talking to your best friend or something?" Liz asked Sarah.

"I *am* talking to my Best Friend," Sarah replied with a grin.

"You know what I mean. Like, you're just *talking*. Naturally. Not worrying about the 'thees' and 'thous.'"

"King James English?" Sarah laughed. "Why Elizabeth, where dost thou gettest the idea that I talketh thus all the timeth?"

Liz smiled. "OK, OK, I get the point. You *don't* talk like that all the time, so you don't talk to Him that way."

"*I* sure don't," said Michael. "I don't think I could if I wanted to."

"Me either," said Sarah. "If I tried to talk like that, it wouldn't be *me* talking, it'd be me trying to be someone else. I don't think God would want that. After all, if He'd wanted me to be someone else, He would've *made* me someone else. He just wants me to be me."

"That makes sense," Liz agreed. "That's good to know, because somehow I used to think I had to talk in some special way to get His attention. Or that He might be there correcting my grammar or something."

"I used to think that, too," Sean admitted. "But then one day I was confessing something to Him, and I was trying to make it all flowery, and—well, I was making excuses, is what it was. Like, if I said it fancy enough, He wouldn't notice that I'd basically fallen flat on my face. So, I'm going on and on about His everlasting mercies and all, and then finally He spoke to me. It wasn't audible, but it was awful darn close. This voice in my head just said, 'Come off it, Sean, just admit that you blew it.' So, I did. I said, 'God, I

Chapter Seventeen

blew it. And I'm sorry.' And before I'd finished the word sorry, He said to me (again in my head) 'Forgiven.' It was so simple, and such a freeing thing, I wished I'd gotten to the point sooner, instead of all that fancy talking in circles, trying to save face."

"So, sometimes He corrects you, like telling you to get to the point?" Liz had vague memories of J's scolding her, mainly for her pessimism or lack of self-respect.

"Yeah, He does, but He's always nice about it. He won't do it just to make me feel bad. He'll always show me what I need to do about it, and it always ends up being a heckuva lot easier to just obey Him than to try and get around it."

"I know what you mean," said Sarah. "I think that's why Jesus said His yoke is easy and His burden is light.'"

"But how many people really *believe* that?" commented Michael.

"Not many," said Sarah and Sean in unison.

"It seems," said Liz, "that Christianity looks a lot different from the inside that it does from the outside. People think of religion and discipline and boring, repetitious prayers. But you guys seem to be having a blast with it." The other three looked at each other and smirked.

"It's kinda like one of those churches with all the stained glass windows," Liz went on. "From the outside, there's this stone structure, all gray and cold-looking, but if you go inside it, especially on a sunny day—"

"—it's gorgeous! Exactly!" exclaimed Sarah. She turned to the others. "Liz is great at finding analogies. "

"That doesn't surprise me," said Sean. "I knew she was a good writer. We were in the same playwriting class, and Liz's skits were always the best."

"Thanks," Liz stammered, surprised by the compliment. "So," She fumbled for the right words "How does one go about . . . you know . . . getting inside?"

There was a long pause, as the other three looked at each other as if to say, *"Does she mean what I think she means?"*

"You mean having a relationship with Jesus?" asked Sarah.

"Well, yeah, I *think* that's what I mean. Actually, I think I may already *have* a relationship with Him, but it's hard to explain." *Sheesh!* she thought. *Why can't I ever do things the normal way?*

"You mean," said Michael, "you just want to be *sure* you're saved?"

"Yeah, I *guess* that's what I mean . . ."

"Do you believe that you're a sinner?" The bluntness of the question caught her off guard, but the recent return of the tangled memories had left no doubt.

"Yeah, I am," she said quietly.

"Do you believe that Jesus died for your sins?"

"Yes. Definitely."

"And that He rose again?"

"Of course," she said, feeling J's presence. "I know He's alive today."

"Then you just pray," said Michael, "and tell Him you're sorry for your sins, and ask Him to come into your heart and be your Savior and Lord and make you into all He wants you to be."

"That's *it*?"

"That's it."

"But . . . that's so simple."

"I know," Michael grinned. "So simple a lot of people miss it. Weird, huh?"

"Yeah, real weird. I guess it's human nature to want to complicate things. It does seem like there should be more to it than that."

"Oh, there is," said Sarah. "A lot more. The salvation experience is just the beginning, but too many people let Satan do a number on them, and then they get all hung up on 'Am I *really* saved?' And they fall into the trap of trying to earn their salvation, so that they never get around to enjoying the salvation that's been given to them free."

It took a moment for Sarah's statement to sink in, but once it did, Liz commented, "What a shame."

"Sure is."

Just then the waitress brought their sundaes. When she had set them all down and left, Sean asked, "Who wants to pray?" Sarah

Chapter Seventeen

and Michael opened their mouths to speak, but something stopped them short. There was a brief, awkward pause.

"I will," said Liz. The others, surprised, looked at each other uncertainly and bowed their heads. Anyone watching Sarah would have seen her lips moving silently.

"Dear Lord," Liz began hesitantly, "thanks for this evening. It was fun . . . and enlightening. Thanks for the good time, and the friends, and this food." She paused and took a deep breath. Her voice was shaky, but she continued. "Lord, I'm a sinner. And I need You. Please come into my heart and be my Savior and my Lord. Make me what You want me to be. Amen."

Liz hesitated, her head still bowed, waiting for the bolt of lightening to hit; it didn't. She wondered if she had "done it right." But when she raised her head, three friends were smiling at her, their faces beaming.

Chapter Eighteen

"Where's Gretl?" the director snapped.

Uh-oh, a child's not paying attention again.

"I'll find her!" Liz volunteered, hurrying out to the greenroom. As the "eldest daughter," she'd found herself feeling responsible for the youngest ones, who of course were not university students but local children. Three little girls had been chosen from at least one hundred at auditions. They had talent, but little experience. Their mothers were present for every rehearsal, but they didn't have much experience, either, and sometimes were found talking among themselves instead of listening for their daughters' cues. Since such small performers were seldom seen in the university theater department, this director was not accustomed to dealing with people with small bladders and short attention spans.

Soon Liz had the tot in her arms, ready for the next scene.

"OK, a little reminder," said the director, his irritation thinly veiled behind a kindergarten-teacher voice. "This is a *run-through*. That means *no stops*. We all need to be where we're supposed to be. OK?" The little girl apparently knew this admonition was for her, for Liz felt the tiny hands grip her a little tighter.

Counselor

"It's his own fault," said Wesley Matthews during the break. "He's the one that picked a play with all these brats in it." Liz cringed and looked over to where the three little girls were sitting on the far side of the room, but apparently their mothers had them engrossed in a board game. Although Wesley made a great Father Von Trapp on stage, backstage it was pretty obvious that he didn't like having small children under foot, so they kept their distance.

"Actually, that was a pretty shrewd move," observed Sean. "Whenever you get kids from the community, you've automatically sold tickets to Mom and Dad and Grandma and Grandpa and all the aunts, uncles, and cousins. I bet most of the elementary school will be coming to Saturday's matinee. A good clean musical makes a great field trip. That's a lot of money for the department. Besides," he added, grinning at Wesley, "you *know* they're cute!"

Wesley scowled. "Just keep them away from me!"

"Hey, they're *your* children, Captain!" Sean teased. He checked his watch. "OK, guys, time to get back out there." He glanced at his clipboard. "Rolf and Leisl, he wants you to do your number again," he said apologetically.

Liz moaned. She didn't think she could do the dance one more time.

"That's what you get for stepping on my toe," gloated a cocky Rolf.

"Sorry, Steve, I'm exhausted tonight."

"Forgiven," said Steve patting her cheek affectionately as he passed her out the door. Liz shot him a dirty look, which he didn't see but Sean did. He gave her a sympathetic smile.

Having Steve Hunter in the role of the boyfriend had taken a lot of the fun out of the whole experience. He was someone who had a hard time getting a date, not because he wasn't physically attractive (in fact, he frequently landed the "handsome young man" role), but because of his obnoxious personality. Now, with Liz, he had a captive date. They flirted, they sang, they danced, and at the end of their number, they kissed. Liz hated that part. It was hard for her to act like an excited adolescent when all she felt was sheer

Chapter Eighteen

nausea. *Oh well, I guess that's what acting's all about*, she thought. *I should get a Tony for this, though.*

"I think we need to practice more," Steve told Liz later as they were leaving.

"Oh?" Liz was non-committal. "I thought we did OK the second time through."

"'Practice makes perfect,' you know." Steve had the annoying habit of throwing clichés around. "I didn't like the way the understudies laughed when I kissed you," he muttered indignantly.

I didn't like the way you kissed me, thought Liz. She didn't feel like talking; her throat was starting to get sore. *One week till the show; this had better be allergy and not a cold!*

"Tomorrow's Saturday, why don't we do a few run-throughs in the afternoon?" Steve persisted. "One o'clock in the greenroom?"

"Oh, OK, I guess." She was too tired to argue.

"Good! It's a date!"

Liz cringed. *Must he always say that?*

"Good night, Steve." She turned to go her way before he could say or do anything else to annoy her. On the way home she fumbled in her pockets for a tissue.

Oh God, let this be an allergy!

The next morning Liz awoke with a full-blown head cold and a sick feeling of dread in her stomach. She knew from past experience how long this could last—a few days or a week or more. She tried hard not to think of the time she'd had laryngitis and was unable to speak for over a month.

Why? she prayed, but got no immediate answer. She allowed herself the luxury of a good cry, but that only made her head feel as if it were going to explode, so she staggered to the kitchen to make a pot of tea.

A few hours, four pills, and twenty-eight Kleenex's later, the phone rang. It was Steve.

"Hey, where are ya?" (*Where do you think I am?*) "I'm waiting!"

"Oh! I forgot! Listen, I've got a really bad cold, I'm just not feeling up to it today."

"Hey, Lizzie, 'The show must go on!'" *Thanks for the sympathy,* "*Stevie.*"

"You don't want to catch my cold," she warned.

"I haven't had a cold in years!" he boasted.

"Oh, OK, I'll be there. Give me twenty minutes." *Jerk!* she thought as she hung up the phone. She berated herself for not having more backbone. She felt like crying again. She knew she should pray, but she was afraid God was mad at her for the way she felt about Steve, and afraid she'd end up getting mad at God for letting her get sick on the eve of her debut. She decided to call Sarah and blurt out the sad story.

"I *thought* you sounded awful! Poor Liz!" she said with genuine empathy.

"And now I've gotta go practice with Rolf—Mr. Conscientious, We-gotta-practice-more-especially-the-kissing-part."

"He said that?"

"No, but he was thinking it. Trust me, I know this guy."

"Can't you get out of it?"

"Not unless I want to risk having him come over here and try to hold my hand or something. I can just imagine what his 'bedside manner' is like!"

"Well you get right home and rest the minute you're finished. Let your understudy do the rehearsal tonight."

"I don't want the director to be ticked off."

"Liz, that's what understudies are for. He'll be more ticked off if you get one of your whopper cases of laryngitis by next weekend." Sarah had a good memory.

"You've got a point."

"Call the director now, and tell him you're not going to make it tonight."

"OK."

"Promise?"

"Geez, what are you my mother?"

"For now, yeah. Your mom's not here, and I am."

"Thanks, Sarah."

"Don't mention it. I love ya!"

Chapter Eighteen

"Love you, too. See ya later."

Liz wasn't sure the practice with Steve did either of them any good. Her brain seemed as congested as her sinuses, and the short dance seemed to drain what little energy she had right out of her. When they got to the end of the dance and it was time for the kiss, she started to warn Steve again that she had a bad cold, but it was obvious that he'd heard that line before, and it wasn't going to faze him.

Jerk, jerk, JERK!

When Liz got back to the apartment, she had a phone message from Sarah:

"Hey, Liz, hope you're feeling better. Call me when you get back, OK?"

Liz didn't really feel like making a phone call, but she knew Sarah was considerate; she wouldn't have asked if she didn't have a good reason.

"Oh good, you're back," came Sarah's cheery voice. "I've got something for you, can I come over?"

"Uh, sure, I'll be here the rest of the day."

"Good. I'll be right over."

A short time later, Sarah showed up with a large kettle of homemade chicken soup.

"It's my mom's prescription," she explained, setting it down on the stove. "One bowlful every two hours." She searched the cupboards for a bowl and grabbed the largest one she could find.

"Hey, thanks, Sarah, you didn't have to do that."

"I know. If I'd *had* to, it wouldn't have been any fun. Now get in bed!"

Liz obediently changed into a robe. She emerged from the bathroom as Sarah was setting on the bedside table a tray containing a large bowl of piping hot soup, a glass, a pitcher of ice water, and a box of tissues.

"Thanks, Sarah. I'd forgotten what a good nurse you are—and a good friend."

"Can the mush and get into bed!" Sarah barked in her best drill-sergeant voice.

"Yes ma'am." Liz was more than glad to obey. As Sarah tucked her in and poured her a glass of water, Liz grew pensive. She hesitated a moment, watching as Sarah plumped the pillows, then said timidly, "Sarah?"

"Hm?" said Sarah, turning to the window and closing the blinds.

"Do you think God's punishing me?" Sarah turned toward her, puzzled.

"Good grief, for what?"

"Well, when my English prof got laryngitis, I was pretty glad about it."

"Glad she was sick, or glad you could go to IV?"

"That I could go to IV."

"Of course! You didn't wish anything bad on your prof, and you had nothing to do with her being sick. Besides, God doesn't work that way. He doesn't sit there watching people and saying, 'I don't think I like what you just did. Here, take that! Ha! Measles! Oh, so you want to make fun of that blind person, well how do you feel about losing your contact lens?' Liz, the prof probably would've gotten sick anyway. The timing was just part of the big picture. 'All things work together for good to those who love the Lord.'"

"You've quoted that before. Where is it?"

"Romans. And don't worry, this cold of yours will turn out OK, too, just trust the Lord with it. And," she picked up her purse to go, "if you need anything, just call Sister Sarah. I *mean* it. You've got a show to get well for. You know that expression—'The show must go on'?"

"Oh, don't say that," Liz groaned with a smile.

"Well, then just take care of yourself, OK?"

"OK."

"Remember, a bowl every two hours, at least."

"Yes ma'am."

"You'll feel like you're floating away, but you'll get better!"

"*OK!*" Liz laughed, shooing her away.

"I'll be over to nag you some more tomorrow. That's part of the treatment, too."

Chapter Eighteen

"Oh great."

"Love ya. 'Bye." And Sarah was gone.

I love you, too, Liz replied silently. What a friend. Of course, Sarah was just living her faith, as usual.

Lord, make me that kind of friend, she prayed.

Chapter Nineteen

The rest of that weekend Liz rested, feeding both her body and her soul. With a bowl of Sarah's soup ever on one side of her bed and her Bible on the other, she followed Sarah's "prescription" and read and prayed and napped.

At times Liz got a warm, happy feeling, out of the blue, and she thought she could actually feel her strength start to come back. She couldn't explain it, but she was grateful.

Sarah called her on Sunday afternoon to see how she was, to ask if she needed anything, and to pray for Liz over the phone, something Liz had never heard of before. She had a mental picture of someone passing Sarah and overhearing her talking to God—on the phone—and wondering what strange kind of cult she belonged to. But of course, Sarah was just doing what came naturally, and letting Liz listen in. And, as Sarah prayed, Liz felt one of those surges of love and strength, and she thought she now knew where they came from—someone had been praying for her. She knew Sarah had prayed for her many times without her knowing it. Had Sarah's prayers had anything to do with her discovering Jesus? There was still so much about prayer that she didn't know, but just spending that weekend in bed, doing the best she could as a "babe in

Christ," as Sarah had affectionately called her, she was beginning to understand that prayer was a two-way thing, that sometimes in the quiet moments of the night, even in times of pain and loneliness and frustration, it's actually easier to hear the "still, small voice." She could almost be thankful she had caught that cold. And she probably *would* be thankful—as soon as she was over it.

OK, Lord, I'm trusting You . . . OK, I'm trying to trust You. I know that "all things work together for good" for me, and I know You know what You're doing . . . She recalled something else she had read about a bewildered would-be follower of Christ.

I believe. Help my unbelief!

And then something—or Someone—told her that was enough for now.

Monday's run-through—or rather, walk-through—was for the sake of the technicians. Lighting was fine-tuned and microphones placed and tested. The cast merely walked through the blocking for the sake of the lighting crew and sang only enough of each song to set the volume levels. Most of Liz and Steve's dance number was skipped. The director figured any freshman could run a spotlight, and any potential problems could be noted during tech and dress rehearsals. All in all, it was a short night, and Liz got to bed relatively early. She was feeling much better, though still a little weak, and remembered to thank the Lord for the easy rehearsal as she happily climbed into bed. She slept soundly all night, except for a split-second dream the moment before waking. In it, she saw the Commons, filled with people, every chair taken except one. It stood empty at a table for two, across from a handicapped student who quietly sat, waiting, ignored by the crowd. A moment later, he turned and looked right at Liz expectantly. Her heart leapt.

With a little gasp, Liz opened her eyes and looked at the clock. She was an hour early waking up. Ordinarily she would have thought, *Good, another hour,* and rolled over to sleep some more, but today she knew better. With her Friend's expectant look still fresh in her mind, she took her Bible and sat by the window, where she and Jesus conversed as though He were sitting across the table

Chapter Nineteen

from her. Actually, He was closer than that. When the alarm went off, Liz felt as refreshed as if she had slept another five hours.

Tuesday night's dress rehearsal had some bugs in it, mostly having to do with the little girls and their mothers. But after Wednesday night off, there would be another dress rehearsal to get everything straightened out, then the big weekend. Steve seemed quieter on Tuesday night and was downright tolerable; he left without any annoying words to Liz. Wednesday night Liz attended a Bible study with Sarah and some of the students from IV, where they all prayed for her performance. Of course, they first gave thanks that Liz had recovered without any complications. "Thanks to Sarah and Jesus!" Liz testified.

"But not necessarily in that order," Sarah hastened to add.

Aaron Hurley was one of those students who seemed to fade into the scenery. Although he was tall and not unattractive, he was extremely quiet. In fact, as Liz had never had any classes with him, she wasn't sure she had ever actually heard him speak before; Aaron seemed to be more of a listener. Unlike many of the students, who were from the greater Chicago area, Aaron was from a rural farming community in the southern part of the state. Ever since early in his freshman year, when it was discovered that he favored country music over rock and rap, he'd been dubbed "Country Boy" and subjected to occasional teasing, which he always took with good-natured resignation. But most of the time his name was rarely mentioned, and he was virtually unknown to the backstage gossips. He had never had a girlfriend that anyone was aware of, had never landed a major role, had never done anything outrageous to distinguish himself. He seemed to keep to himself and mind his own business, and that seemed to be fine with everyone else.

So, it was with mild surprise that Liz saw him Thursday night in Rolf's costume. He was about the same height as Steve, but thinner. He had removed his glasses for the rehearsal, and his eyes, large and wide-set, made him look younger than he was. His sandy brown hair had been slicked back, and the uniform he wore was so unlike his usual jeans and flannel shirt that he was scarcely recognizable as "Country Boy." Standing awkwardly with his hands in his pockets, he seemed nervous and self-conscious; Steve was nowhere in sight.

"OK, everybody, listen up!" the director barked. "Tonight again it's straight run-through. Any problems we'll fix between now and tomorrow night, so just keep going! Tonight, and probably tomorrow night, we're using the understudy for Rolf." Someone mumbled a question, the director muttered, "Sick as a dog. He's not going anywhere for a while." Then he raised his voice and continued, "OK, now I don't want anyone else getting sick and losing their voice, OK?"

"Your cold was pretty potent, I guess," commented a "nun" with a wry smile.

"Hey, I warned him," said Liz defensively, but the other girl's chuckle told her she understood; her smirk seemed to say, *It serves him right.*

Liz thought Aaron did the dance number quite well for his first time doing it with her; he had always practiced with her understudy before. Although he held her more lightly than Steve did, and there was a slight tremor in his hands that only Liz detected, he knew every step. Even the director seemed impressed. But when it came to the moment of the kiss, Rolf suddenly looked flustered, and as Liz looked into his eyes uncertainly, he impulsively kissed her on the forehead. The cast backstage exploded into laughter; Liz blushed.

Two hours later, the cast and crew gathered on stage for the director's notes. It was an interesting assortment of characters of all shapes and sizes, everything from nuns to Nazis, from formal dinner party guests to tiny refugees. All seemed tired, but happy— all except Aaron, who looked very sheepish. "Here it comes," he groaned. Liz hoped he wouldn't get too much hassle about the non-kiss.

"Nuns, your song sounded better, but I think you can project even more. Remember, singing's probably one of the few things these ladies do all day. And you need to clear out faster after Scene

Chapter Nineteen

One. And stage crew, watch for their habits. I kept thinking one of them was going to catch on the corner of a flat and cause a disaster.

"Children, try to pay attention to Miss Maria, OK? Don't be looking around at other things. And go easy jumping on that bed, we don't want it collapsing." He looked at the little girls until he was reasonably certain they'd heard and understood. Then he glanced back down at his notes.

"Rolf!" The director looked up with an expression that couldn't be interpreted right away. Aaron held his breath.

"Good dancing. Nice job on the song, too. Oh, about that kiss . . ." The cast chuckled; Aaron stiffened, red-faced. There was a tense pause.

". . . I liked it that way. It was perfect. Keep it." The actor breathed a sigh of relief. Liz smiled and wondered if it would be terribly evil of her to pray that Steve would have a slow recovery.

Chapter Twenty

"I thought you said God didn't work that way," Liz said to Sarah the next day. They were sitting at a table in the Commons with Sean and Michael. "He sure seems to have zapped Steve, though."

"Well, there is such a thing as consequences, you know."

"How'd you get so smart, Sarah?" Liz was still in awe of her friend's wisdom.

"I've had a few consequences myself." Sarah replied with a smile.

"I remember when I finally got the understudy for a major part," Liz said, "I really wanted a shot at it, but it never happened. It wouldn't have seemed right to pray for someone to get sick or something. But if they had, and I'd gotten to play the part, I would've been glad. Is that wrong?"

"I've wrestled with that myself," Sean said. "At tryouts, I'd always pray so hard that I'd get the part. And I'd usually get understudy, which was better than nothing, but still a little disappointing. I actually understudied for Steve once." Liz had a hard time picturing that; Sean resembled Steve about as much as a root beer float resembled milk of magnesia.

"I especially struggled because I never really liked Steve, and it was hard not to resent the guy. I prayed about it a lot—not to get the part, but to just not be jealous, 'cause it was only hurting me. I mean, I'd see him and he'd make some cocky remark and I'd get mad for the rest of the day!" He smiled a little sheepishly. "Now I'm *still* praying about my attitude, 'cause I feel like he got what he deserved, and it's hard not to gloat." Liz suppressed a smirk; she knew exactly what he meant.

"Being godly's harder than I thought," she said. "All this attitude stuff . . . motives. I never realized how much crud is in me before."

Opening night brought an assortment of feelings: the newness of actually having a "real part," the nervousness of knowing how many strangers and friends would fill the auditorium, and the impatience to just get out there and do it. She was sharing a dressing room with two other people: Amber, who had landed the part of Baroness Schroeder, and Audrey Mayfield, a voice major from the opera department who had the part of the Reverend Mother. It was a little different, and much quieter, than being a member of the chorus. After having spent so many hours in the past helping others with their makeup and costumes in such a setting, it seemed strange to be the one being helped. A shy freshman named Emily was French braiding Liz's hair, and the Reverend Mother was pacing the floor doing vocal warm-ups when there was a knock at the door. Amber, who was closest to the door, laid her eyeliner down and opened the door a crack.

"OK, thanks," she said pulling a long, white floral box into the room.

"Liz?" she sang in a teasing voice. "It's for you!"

Me? Liz's heart skipped a beat as déjà vu hit. *Oh, probably from Mom and Dad,* she told herself; she had enough to be nervous about right now, thank you. She took the box, opened it, and separated the folds of green tissue. Her heart warmed at the sight of a single large red rose, nestled in a bed of ferns.

"How sweet!" exclaimed the Reverend Mother. "Who's it from?"

"Probably my Mom and Dad," Liz said, not very convincingly.

"Probably?" teased Amber.

Chapter Twenty

Liz took out the card and read,

Congratulations on your debut!
Relax and have fun, you'll do great!
P.S. You are loved.

No signature. That's not like Mom and Dad.
Liz's cheeks felt hot as she stammered, "I need to put this in water." She found a Coke bottle for the job and rinsed and filled it at the sink. As she placed the rose in the bottle, the ferns branched out, surrounding the rose like handmaidens around a queen. There was another knock at the door.

"Five minutes to curtain!" came Sean's voice from the other side. And with a rustle of black linen, Reverend Mother was gone.

As Emily finished braiding her hair, Liz could hear the orchestra begin the overture through the dressing room speakers. The butterflies fluttered again at the thought of running out on stage with an actual audience this time. Or was it because of the reflected elegance of the rose and the mystery behind it? She had a flashback from a distant dream—the image of a dozen crimson roses bursting through green tissue, a note written in a shaky hand, and her mind began to wander. She sat staring at the face of "Leisl," her powder brush poised at her cheek.

The voice of Colleen Thompson—Maria—roused her from her daydream. Colleen, as usual, sounded confident and professional, and Liz had to admit that she liked to hear her sing; she was a natural. But Liz knew that the lovely song about the music of the mountains was in reality not being sung in the serenity of an Alpine hillside, but on stage, in front of a packed house.

Now it wasn't butterflies, it was bats. As she took her first costume off the rack, she noticed that her hands were shaking. The realization hit: *This is it.* She had dreamed for so long of having a significant part, how wonderful and exciting it would be, and now she was petrified. The fleeting thought of an old nightmare came like the attack of a familiar enemy. What if she went out there and forgot everything? She looked around to see if anyone else had noticed her jangled nerves, but Emily was busy straightening the makeup, and the Baroness was absorbed in a magazine, chewing her gum conspicuously.

Help me, Jesus, she prayed. *I'm scared.* Well, it was a prayer that was definitely to the point, and she felt a little better. Sarah had once told her that courage isn't being unafraid, it was doing what one had to do, in spite of fear—or in her case, stark terror. She hoped that this was true, for the backstage jitters had certainly arrived.

She slipped on the white culottes and asked Amber to help her with the top—a white, slipover sailor blouse with a large collar, just asking to be smudged with makeup. Amber laid down the magazine and walked over.

"So . . . ya scared?" *Speaking of to-the-point*, Liz thought.

"Yeah, kind of . . . no, *very*."

"Don't worry, you'll do great. Just pretend it's another rehearsal, and if that doesn't work, picture the audience in their underwear. Works for me."

"Thanks, I'll remember that. Have you heard who's Rolf tonight?"

"No, but I haven't seen Steve all day. Maybe you'll luck out." The girls chuckled, Amber with sadistic amusement, Liz out of sheer nervousness. Amber straightened Liz's collar and gave her a swat on the seat.

"There ya go, knock 'em dead."

Liz lined up with the other children awaiting their entrance in the wings, illuminated only by the light that spilled over from the stage. She couldn't tell if anyone else was scared, but she noticed Sean whispering something to the littlest one. When Liz caught his eye, he gave her a wink and a "thumbs up." She folded her hands and pleadingly mouthed the words, "Pray for me!" He smiled reassuringly and gave her the "OK" sign. She returned his smile; she had a feeling he was praying for her already, and this calmed her a bit.

At the shrill blowing of the Captain's whistle, the children ran in, lined up, and came to attention. When it was Liz's turn to speak,

Chapter Twenty

she was relieved to find that the lines were indeed still there. This was a good sign; it meant she wasn't going to "lose it." But it also meant this was reality, not a nightmare; she wasn't going to wake up, so she had to keep going.

But any nervousness that may have shown at first was probably fitting anyway for an adolescent facing a stern father and a new governess at the same time. As Liz realized she was not seriously blowing it, she began to relax and enjoy the play. She was encouraged by an advantage she had discovered in having a role with many scenes: if one messed up at the beginning, one had the rest of the play to redeem oneself.

When Rolf appeared and Liz saw that it was Aaron, her face lit up in delight, which was also fitting for that point in the plot. But the audience had no idea that it was for a reason entirely separate from good acting. Her eyes met his, and as he read her smile, he responded in kind. An Oscar-winning performance of young love in bloom? No, just evidence that Steve was still sick.

The song and dance went without a hitch, except that for a moment Liz thought Rolf was going to kiss her on the lips, but he apparently remembered the director's instructions in time. She hoped it would go as well the next night, when her parents would be there.

Then again, Steve might get his voice back.

Backstage, Emily sprinkled Liz with water before her next entrance—a climb in the window out of the rain. It was tricky, since Emily had to use enough water to make it obvious that Liz was wet, and yet not so much that her makeup would run or her hair take too long to dry for the next scene. As Emily carefully dribbled the water down Liz's braid and onto her costume, Liz found herself thinking, *This is so much fun! Maybe I could do this for a living!* Every time a line got a laugh it was exhilarating, and when the audience broke into applause, it was a rush she hadn't experienced since high school. Off stage, changing costumes, she was impatient to get back out and do some more.

"This one's my favorite," she said as she donned the bridesmaid's dress for the brief wedding scene. The different costumes gave her opportunity to express different moods and facets of her personality. This one was a pale aqua gown with an abundance of chiffon and a wide satin belt. In it, Liz felt graceful and elegant, and moved accordingly.

"It *is* gorgeous," said Emily as she zipped up the back for her.

Amber looked up from her magazine. "Yeah," she added cynically, "U of I teaches you everything except how to run a theater on a budget." The Chicago girl was working her way through school, and made all her own clothes, so Liz understood where her cynicism was coming from.

As Emily pinned tiny flowers in Liz's hair, Amber must have seen her eyes drifting toward the Coke bottle vase, because her next comment was, "So, Liz, dj'ya figure out who sent the rose yet?"

"No, I really have no idea."

"Maybe it was Wesley."

"Wesley?"

"Yeah, I think he still has the hots for you."

"Gee, you make it sound so romantic."

Liz *had* thought she had detected a look in Wesley's eyes as he sang "Edelweiss," a look of fondness and affection as his eyes met hers. But then, as he was the father, he was supposed to look at his children that way. And backstage he seemed cocky as ever, so Amber's suggestion seemed far-fetched at best.

"Nah . . . I don't think a rose is exactly his M.O."

"Ya got a point there . . . Hey!" exclaimed Amber in sudden recollection. "Weren't you doodling J's all over your notebook a while back? You never did tell me who *that* was, but maybe it's from him."

"No, it couldn't . . . that's . . . impossible."

"Oh." Amber seemed disappointed that Liz still wasn't explaining the "J" thing. *Oh well, let her wonder,* Liz thought, grabbing a plastic bouquet from the prop table.

"Gotta run!"

"OK. Enjoy the wedding."

And Liz did. She enjoyed the rest of the show, although she was impatient for the next one, and being in the spotlight again for

Chapter Twenty

her solo. By now she was confident and loving every minute of the experience. The curtain calls were a first for her, first since high school, at least. As she and Aaron joined hands and trotted downstage for their bow, the applause grew louder, and Liz got another rush. It didn't matter that as Colleen and Wesley took their bows the applause grew louder still. As the cast joined hands and bowed together, the audience rose to its feet, and Liz felt sheer exhilaration at being part of the whole wonderful thing.

Liz, Amber, and Audrey burst back into the dressing room together to begin the ritual of getting out of their costumes and makeup.

"*Awesome* singing, Audrey!" Liz gushed, slipping off her shawl and handing it to Emily.

"No kidding!" Amber chimed in. "Every time you sing 'Climb Every Mountain,' my *goose bumps* get goose bumps!"

"Thanks," said Audrey modestly. "You two did great, too."

"Hey, Liz, wouldn't it be great if Steve stayed sick all weekend?" Amber asked with a fiendish grin.

"Fat chance of that," Liz laughed awkwardly. If she had been honest, she would admit that she had thought the same thing. Now that Amber had verbalized it so bluntly and Liz had heard how it sounded, she felt a little guilty.

"Still, it would be nice. You and Aaron make such a cute couple—don't they, Aud?" Amber teased.

The opera student just smiled and began removing the hairpins from her wimple, reluctant to get involved in this discussion. She was saved by a knock at the door.

"Everybody decent?" Amber asked. Not waiting for an answer, she opened the door.

Liz heard Sean's voice say, "Liz?" She stepped out of her shoes and came to the door, where she found Sean, Sarah, Michael, and several other friends from Intervarsity.

"Hi guys! How'd you get back here?" she asked.

Sarah grinned at Sean. "Never underestimate the power of headphones and a clipboard," she declared.

"You *do* look official, Sean," Liz told him with mock awe. Sean just looked smug.

"You did great!" squealed Sarah, giving Liz a big hug that got greasepaint on her white blouse.

"Oh, I'm sorry, Sarah!" cried Liz, grabbing a tissue and trying to blot it off.

"No problem," Sarah assured her. "This is better than an autograph!"

"Seriously," said Michael, "your singing and dancing was . . . *great*!"

"She did do great, didn't she?" agreed the stage manager proudly.

Liz returned the compliment; "And Sean did a great job stage managing, didn't he?" The blank look on the others' faces indicated that they had no idea what a stage manager did, or how they would tell if he had done a good job. "It's one of those jobs that only gets noticed if you mess up," she explained.

"Oh," said Sarah. "I guess you learn something new every day." As Sean and Liz exchanged amused glances, she added, "So, what're you doing now?"

"After I get cleaned up? I hadn't really thought that far."

"We're heading over to Delights," said Michael. "Come on over."

"OK, I'll meet you there. Thanks!"

The group said goodbye and headed out.

"Aren't you going to Wesley's?" Amber asked.

"Wesley's?"

"Yeah, he's having a little cast party, or an afterglow, or whatever."

"And I'm invited?"

"Hello-o-o?" Amber sang. "You're cast!"

"I am!" Liz laughed. "I'm so used to being chorus or tech, I guess it never occurred to me to assume . . ."

"C'mon Liz, you can go to Delights any time. I haven't seen you at a party in ages."

"Well, I suppose . . . OK."

The moment they walked into the crowed apartment, Liz remembered *why* she hadn't been to a party in ages. The myriad people packed into the dimly lit living room were drinking and smoking, neither of which Liz enjoyed; the subtle scent of marijuana hung in the air.

Chapter Twenty

"Liz!" a loud voice greeted her. Wesley stepped through the crowd and gave her a hearty hug. "Glad you could make it!" She could smell liquor on his breath and she had a sudden feeling of déjà vu that frightened her, though she didn't know just why.

"Can I get you a drink?" he asked, loudly but cordially. It still seemed strange to have Wesley treating her nicely, but now that they were in a show together, he seemed to have forgotten any earlier encounters.

"Uh, not just now, thanks."

"Well, the bar's over there, help yourself whenever you're ready. Yo, Dave!" And he was gone. Liz was somewhat relieved that he had left her alone so quickly. She started to say something to Amber, but saw that her friend had taken off and was already socializing, a drink in one hand, cigarette in the other.

Well, this is fun, Liz thought, feeling suddenly very alone in spite of the crowd. Her eyes scanned the dark room for someone she might comfortably talk to. The walls were decorated with posters from various plays: some Broadway musicals, from contemporary to decades old, some comedies, some tragedies, arranged in no apparent order, until Liz realized these were all shows Wesley had played in during his career at the university. Each one, no doubt, had special significance for him; either he was of a sentimental bent, or, more likely, he liked to keep track of his accomplishments and these posters were the theatrical equivalent of notches on a gun. But these were the first "notches" she had ever seen that were framed and displayed with soft lighting. She spotted a rolled-up poster in one corner, awaiting a frame. There was just enough of it showing that she recognized it: *The Sound of Music*. Ah yes, Wesley's next trophy.

"Hi Liz," a familiar voice broke her train of thought.

Startled, she turned and saw Aaron standing there, looking as out of place as she felt. He was leaning against the wall, his hands in his pockets.

"Are we the only sober ones here?" he asked.

"Looks like it," Liz laughed. "I don't think I'll stay long."

"Me neither. The smoke's gettin' to me." After another awkward pause, he added, "You wanna go outside?"

"Sure."

The clear spring night was much more pleasant than the party, and much more conducive to conversation.

"This is much better," Liz said with a sigh of relief. "I felt pretty out of place in there."

"Yeah, I was feelin' like a snow shovel in July myself. So, how'd you enjoy your first big performance?"

"Loved it. And you?"

"Loved it," he answered, smiling. "It's kinda strange not knowin' if I'll be doin' it again or not."

"Oh, I hope you can," Liz said. Seeing the odd look on Aaron's face, she quickly added, "Not that I want Steve to be sick." She paused. Not wanting to be dishonest, she added, "necessarily." Aaron chuckled. "I just . . . it would be nice for you, to be able to do it again. You did a great job." Aaron seemed gratified to hear her say it.

"So did you. I . . . really enjoyed it."

Just then a couple burst through the door, laughing loudly and needling each other with obscenities that made the blood rush to Liz's cheeks.

"I'm pretty tired," she said. "I think I'd better go."

"Can I walk you home?" Aaron asked amicably.

Without thinking, she blurted out, "Oh, that's OK, you don't have to do that." Then, seeing him step back shyly, she added, "Unless you want to."

"Sure," he said. "I don't mind. I've had enough of this party, too."

They walked the four blocks without saying much. The experiences of the evening were sinking in with all their contrasts: the reverent and the profane, the clamor of the party and the stillness of the night, the vast audience, the party crowd, and now, the privacy. One thing was certain: the day had not been boring.

"This is my place," said Liz. "Thanks for walking me home."

Aaron shrugged. "You're welcome." His hands in his pockets, he looked at her with a half-smile and softly began singing "So Long, Farewell."

Chapter Twenty

Liz smiled at him and finished the line.

"See ya tomorrow," Aaron said. Then, with his hands still in his pockets, he turned and walked away.

Chapter Twenty-one

When Liz showed up for the performance the next day, she was greeted by stage manager Sean. He had the characteristic clipboard under his arm, which had become like a regular appendage, and the headphones, unplugged, wrapped around his neck.

"Hey, Liz, what happened to you last night? We missed you!" He didn't ask accusingly, yet Liz felt a sudden pang of guilt.

"Oh, I'm sorry. I was pretty tired and decided to go home." It was true. Well, not the *whole* truth, but Sean hadn't asked for details.

"So, are ya well rested? Two shows today!"

A little thrill of excitement created enough adrenaline to assure that she was fully awake.

"Yeah, I'm feeling pretty good, actually," she said with a smile.

"Good." He gave her a wink and a thumbs up and started to leave.

"Hey, Sean?"

"Yeah?"

"Thanks for the prayers." He gave her a warm grin.

"Any time. And don't thank me, I just send 'em, I don't answer 'em."

As he walked away, Liz thought of Jesus for the first time that day. *Thank You, too*, she prayed. That was all that she had time to say to Him for a while, since she had overslept and was already late for makeup.

When Liz walked into the dressing room, the first thing to catch her eye was the rose. It had opened a little wider and was even more beautiful than when it had first arrived. A bundle was sitting next to it, and when she ripped off the floral paper, she beheld a basket of assorted cut flowers from her parents. So, it seemed very unlikely that they had sent the rose as well. Besides, this arrangement was more their style: an abundance of carnations, daisies, and baby's breath, complete with container and bow. But though it dwarfed the one lone flower in the Coke bottle, the single red blossom persisted in drawing her attention, first from the larger arrangement, then from the task of applying her makeup. It seemed to be winking and playfully teasing her. She found herself smiling wistfully at it, and wondering.

But the show soon took over her conscious thought as she reviewed lines, cues, and choreography, and relating to the other actors. As Leisl, she warmed up to Maria—Colleen—whom she had often envied. She watched Wesley, as the Captain, be transformed from the stern drill-sergeant to affectionate father. She watched him smile warmly at the little girls who backstage had irritated him so; and Liz learned not to take it personally when the same loving gaze was directed her way.

Wesley's skill also inspired her to make the most of the fact that Steve was back, pale and slightly hoarse, but obviously determined not to be replaced permanently. Aaron seemed more than a little let down, seeing that his moment of fame had passed. Liz could feel for him, having herself been pushed aside in the past, but she tried not to let it deter her from performing her best as the giddy teenager who was head-over-heels infatuated with (gulp!) Steve. The audience applauded enthusiastically at the close of their number, and though she didn't enjoy performing with Steve nearly as much as with Aaron, the ovation was still intoxicating.

Later in the evening, the audience for "So Long, Farewell" included the Captain's dinner guests, who watched the children in

Chapter Twenty-one

dignified amusement. One chorus member caught Liz's eye, and although he was now just a face in the crowd, Liz noticed how striking he looked in his tuxedo. He smiled at her as the chorus waved goodbye and sang their one closing line.

Before, he had always been just Aaron Hurley, the shy acting major, much like Liz. He did not fit her idea of the male actor. Her mind had formed a stereotype around the more boisterous, cocky, arrogant young men, who were probably just as insecure as anyone but dealt with their insecurities differently. When she thought of Aaron, Liz realized she had been unfair in her sweeping generalization that nice male actors were harder to find than a parking spot on campus. There were plenty of nice ones; Aaron was proof of that. They just got routinely upstaged by the Steves and the Wesleys.

It was for this reason that Liz was delighted to see Aaron's face at the dressing room door when the performance had ended; she was surprised at just how delighted she was. He was still in his tux, since the chorus had been included in the curtain call, being allowed to take their bows en masse and back out of the way for the cast to come forward.

Aaron's makeup accented his prominent cheekbones, and made his eyes look even larger and darker than usual. Although he was dressed formally, he still leaned against the door frame, his hands in his pockets.

"Nice job," he said with a shy smile that betrayed more sadness than congratulations.

"Thanks," Liz replied, finding herself suddenly shy as well. "I'm sorry you couldn't be Rolf, though."

Aaron shrugged. "That's the breaks. I got to do one show, though; that's better'n most understudies ever get to do."

Liz had to agree. She knew from bitter experience that most actors will make it to a performance if they have to dance on a broken leg, rather than let the understudy replace them even for one night. Liz would have been very surprised if Steve *hadn't* come back.

Counselor

There was an awkward pause, as neither Liz nor Aaron could think of anything else to say. Aaron's gaze drifted over to the mirror, where his eyes fixed on the rose, now in full bloom.

"Isn't that gorgeous?" Liz said wistfully, staring at it herself.

Aaron didn't answer right away, and when she looked back at him, Liz could see, even through his makeup, that his face was quite red.

"I . . . gotta go," he said suddenly, and before Liz could answer, he had retreated to the chorus members' dressing room. A thought came to her.

"You don't suppose . . . ?" she began.

"Hmm?" said Amber, but when Liz looked over, the Baroness was preoccupied with the pins in her hair. Audrey had left the room.

"Never mind," Liz murmured absently as she sat down to take off her makeup.

Suddenly, Amber snapped, "Liz, what are you doing?!"

"What?" Liz replied, startled.

"It's Saturday matinee." Liz registered a blank. "Kids . . . autographs? Hello-o-o?"

"Oh! That's right! I totally forgot!"

The children always showed up at the matinee in droves, and these were undoubtedly the most enthusiastic audience members. It was traditional for the cast members to appear in the lobby afterward in full costume to sign autographs.

"Well, let's get going. You're one of the ones they're really going to want—Miss Sixteen-Going-on-Seventeen." She snapped her gum and winked. "You little Barbie Doll, you!" she added with a grin, pinching Liz's cheek.

"Ow! All right! I'm coming!"

Liz wasn't prepared for the response of the children, since she had never been in this position before. When she emerged from backstage, a high-pitched voice squealed "Leisl!" and a cluster of little girls soon surrounded Liz, clutching their programs and waiting for her to sign them. They stared, giggled, and asked preadolescent questions such as, "Does Rolf kiss you backstage, too?" to

Chapter Twenty-one

which Liz just smiled, not daring to speak any of the answers that came to mind.

She saw Rolf at the other end of the lobby, basking in the temporary glory of stardom, ignoring that this juvenile idol worship was based on the immaturity of persons who are at an age at which looks are everything.

But, truth be told, Liz felt it, too: a rush of confidence and self-esteem that didn't usually come so easily. With the adoring eyes of these children on her, their shy questions and giggling response to her answers, she felt that at last she was important enough for someone to take notice. She thought of people she wished could see her now—Liz Danfield, signing autographs! *I could get used to this*, she thought.

One little girl wanted to have her picture taken with Liz, and the moment the camera flashed, every little girl in the place fairly stampeded to be in a picture with "big sister," too. Liz put her arms around dozens of children that afternoon and smiled her sweetest, knowing that, for a moment anyway, she was a kind of role model.

When the last child had waved goodbye, Liz headed for the dressing room to change for dinner, still feeling quite edified from all the attention, and completely forgetting where it was that she was supposed to be getting her self-worth.

By the time she had slipped back into her jeans and T-shirt, Sean told her that her parents were there to see her. Surprised that they had already arrived, she ran to greet them, thank them for the flowers, and try to talk them into taking her someplace fast for dinner instead of a five-star restaurant.

"I just don't want to be late getting back. It's such a tight schedule," she explained apologetically, not wanting to appear ungrateful, but also not wanting to attempt her song and dance immediately after having stuffed herself with shrimp cocktail and prime rib.

"It's OK, darling!" Rachel exclaimed. "You do what you need to do."

"That's right," said George. "We're here mainly to see your performance. Maybe if there's a nice place to eat around here, your mother and I can . . ."

"No we can't, George," said Rachel firmly. "*We* don't want to be late, either!"

"There's a place in the Student Union that serves salads and stuff," said Liz. "We could probably get something quick there."

"That would be fine, dear," said Rachel quickly, before anyone had a chance to suggest a plan B and complicate things. The three walked to the Commons and sat down to a brief but adequate meal. Then Liz headed back to get dressed.

The Saturday night audience was altogether different from those of Friday night and the matinee. Friday's audiences tended to be quieter, showing an "I'm tired. Entertain me" attitude. Saturday's matinee was full of children who were warm and receptive. But, although Saturday night's audience responded with enthusiasm, their laughter and applause came at different times and intensities from the others. It fascinated Liz that an audience could have its own personality, and she highly suspected that most audience members were oblivious to the important role they played in a production. After all, they were a major reason many of the graduates from the department would stay in live theater instead of going into movies or television.

The end of Act I was one of the moments that Liz always relished. Audrey had a magnificent voice, and though most of the actors weren't that "into" opera, a well-known song like "Climb Every Mountain," sung in a voice the caliber of Audrey's was breathtaking. Most of the cast and crew would leave their card games backstage to stand in the wings and listen to Audrey sing. Liz was always among the first ones there, craning her neck to see, and luxuriating in the goose bumps she always experienced. Saturday night was no different; as everyone began crowding together to enjoy the moment, Liz was oddly aware of the person next to her. She glanced over and realized it was Aaron. She smiled warmly at him and he smiled back shyly, immediately returning his gaze to the stage. As more people moved into the small space, she felt the brush of Aaron's shoulder, and his hand inadvertently touching hers. Out of the corner of her eye, she could see that he was standing stiffly in the light that spilled over from the stage, his eyes

Chapter Twenty-one

fixed on Audrey, but his mind obviously somewhere else. Liz froze, not moving her hand, not knowing what was happening, or whether anything was happening at all. As they stood listening to the gorgeous melody and passionate rendition of the song, her heart was pounding. As the orchestra and soloist brought the song to its climax, it seemed her emotions were reaching a crescendo of their own. Was it the power of the music, or was there something more?

As Audrey passionately sang the final lines, admonishing Maria to pursue her dream, Liz felt Aaron's fingers entwined with hers. He squeezed her hand, and though she didn't squeeze his in return, neither did she pull away. She simply stood there, weak-kneed, not daring to look in his direction, and she was reasonably sure he wasn't looking at her, either. Feeling like the inexperienced adolescent she was playing, she wished she could just go home and think this over.

The audience predictably exploded into applause at Audrey's finish, and the stage went dark for a moment. Aaron's hand slipped away and when the lights came up, he was already headed for the greenroom. He paused and glanced back through the crowd, his face flushed and his eyes questioning fearfully. Liz smiled affectionately, and he smiled back, seeming both relieved and delighted; then he was gone.

In Liz's mind, the pieces were beginning to come together. So the rose *was* from Aaron! She smiled at the thought of discovering who the "secret admirer" was. She was certain that in the darkness, with all eyes on Audrey, no one else could have seen what transpired in that brief moment of revelation.

But she was wrong.

Chapter Twenty-two

The rest of the show that night was a blur. Liz recited her lines on cue, but her thoughts were divided, and she had neither the intensity nor energy level of previous performances. Yet the audience responded with enthusiasm to the production as a whole, and curtain calls went on longer than usual, possibly because it was an energetic Saturday night audience. Liz and Steve were allowed to come forward for an extra bow, as were Audrey, Colleen, and Wesley. Liz found herself wishing that Aaron had been the one taking the bows with her again. Having been mortified to learn that Steve had actually argued with the director over the revision of the kiss, she was more disgusted with him than ever. And, the revelation of Aaron's feelings for her earlier had given her an almost adolescent desire to share such a moment—or *any* moment—with him.

He showed up at her dressing room door afterward, exhibiting the same shy smile Liz was growing very fond of.

"So . . . ya wanna do somethin'?" he asked, then added with mock enthusiasm, "Hey, I hear there's a big cast party!"

"Oh, *man!*" said Liz with equal sarcasm. "I'm gonna have to miss it! My parents are here. They probably want to take me somewhere for dessert or something before they head back."

"They come far?"

"St. Louis."

"You're from St. Louis?"

"Guilty."

"Wow, City Girl," said Country Boy. "What part?"

"Ladue."

He seemed suddenly intimidated. "Wow, *rich* City Girl!"

"Hey, Hon - great job!" George Danfield's voice boomed down the hall. He strode over and gave his daughter a big bear hug.

"Thanks, Dad," said Liz, hugging him back. "Where's Mom?"

"Oh, she's in the lobby. You know your mother, didn't think it proper to come traipsing back here without a formal invitation. But I met that young man with the clipboard, kinda looked like he was in charge, and I asked him."

Liz could see Sean close by, talking with some stage hands. He glanced her way and winked without a break in his instructions.

"Well, I still need to change and get my makeup off, so tell Mom I'll be up in about ten"—she glanced at Aaron—"fifteen minutes."

"Fine, fine," said George, looking inquisitively at the young man in the tuxedo who apparently had nothing better to do than stand by his daughter.

"Oh! Dad, this is Aaron Hurley. He played the part of Rolf Friday night when Steve was sick."

George put out his hand. "Good to meet you, son."

"Good to meet *you,* Sir."

George's face registered a delight that was perceptible only to Liz, and she was pleased that Aaron had scored points with her father already; George loved to have young people call him "Sir."

After a moment's pause in which George seemed to be further sizing up the actor, he said abruptly, "Well! I'll go tell your mother that you'll be up in ten"—he glanced at Aaron—"fifteen minutes."

"OK, Dad, see ya in a bit."

Chapter Twenty-two

"Goodbye, Mr. Danfield."

"So," began Aaron when George had left, "one more performance, huh?"

"Yeah, this weekend's really going fast. It'll be over before we know it," Liz said wistfully. "I don't think I'll ever forget the experience, though."

Aaron's brown eyes met hers, and he said softly, "I know I'll never forget this weekend." Liz smiled. She wished she didn't have to say goodbye to him yet.

"Hey Aaron, would you like to go to church with me tomorrow? My friends told me about this church where a lot of the college students go, and they're taking me in the morning."

Aaron was hesitant. "I'm pretty tired. I think I'm gonna sleep in tomorrow. You know—big weekend," he said sheepishly.

"I know what you mean. I overslept this morning. Well, keeping your energy up is important. You never know," she smiled mischievously, "Steve might get sick again."

She couldn't tell whether the gleam in his eye came from malicious wishful thinking, or just delight that the same thought had occurred to Liz that had occurred to him.

"Well, I'm not gonna hold my breath," he chuckled. "But thanks."

They stood smiling at each other; there was so much to be said, yet both of them were, for the moment, speechless.

Finally, Aaron said with a slight sigh, "Well, have fun with your parents."

"Thanks. See ya tomorrow."

Aaron's face brightened. "Yeah, see ya tomorrow."

Liz decided to introduce her parents to Delights; she knew they probably wouldn't have appreciated the atmosphere at some of the other places students hung out late at night. But ice cream seemed to be the perfect finish for the evening. George would have liked more than he ordered, but as Rachel was the official cholesterol counter, her word stood firm.

As they waited for their order, George and Rachel raved about the show. Liz was glad she was able to be in a relatively old show

Counselor

that her parents' generation understood and enjoyed. They, of course, expressed particular admiration for their daughter's performance, especially her song and dance with that handsome young man who played the boyfriend. When Liz's facial expression involuntarily soured at the mention of Steve, her parents questioned her response. Not wanting to be unkind, she simply said, "I enjoyed doing the scene with the understudy better."

"Oh, that young man I met outside the dressing room?" George asked.

"Yes. Aaron Hurley."

"He seemed like a *very* nice young man!"

"He is," Liz smiled.

Rachel for a moment looked as though she regretted having waited in the lobby; had she missed something? Although she had been careful to "respect Liz's space" and allow her time to be with her friends, Rachel momentarily was having second thoughts.

As the conversation went on about the show, school, and Liz's friends, all three noticed that Aaron's name came up repeatedly. Although no one actually came out and questioned or stated anything about his exact relationship to Liz, George and Rachel were not too old to recognize love in a young person's eyes. It gave them plenty to talk about on the way home.

Chapter Twenty-three

    Liz found the final performance Sunday afternoon to be a much more emotional experience than she had expected. Along with the thrill of performing came the sad realization at the close of each scene that this was the last time she would ever be performing that particular scene with those particular people. Even dancing with Steve had a bittersweet quality about it.

    Aaron again stood by Liz backstage for Audrey's final solo, and this time he dared to slip his arm around her waist; she responded in kind. In this way the two remained for the duration of the song and together were inspired to climb mountains, ford streams, and follow rainbows. It was corny, to be sure, but this was one of those times the entire company allowed itself to partake in a binge of sentimentality. The seniors especially were carried away by the moment, as they were preparing to climb mountains in pursuit of their own dreams—these mountains being mainly in New York and Hollywood. For the two who stood with arms around each other, who were already prone to the romantic, it seemed like a moment ordained by heaven. At the final notes of the solo, as if on cue, Liz laid her head on Aaron's shoulder, and he gently kissed the auburn curls. A split second later, however, they were standing erect and clapping along with the rest. For although the relaxed Sunday afternoon audience responded with moderate enthusiasm, the "audience" behind the scenes, who had grown increasingly appreciative of the song and its singer, broke out in wild applause, hoots, and whistles, that simultaneously flattered and embarrassed the soloist.

Before Liz knew it, she was taking her final bow, and though the applause was polite and somewhat gratifying, it was anticlimactic after Saturday's audiences. More than that, Liz had an uncomfortable knot in her stomach at the realization that this was the end of the show. Not only would she be denied the thrill of playing the part again—with memorized lines and predictable outcome—but now she would be forced to focus her attention on the very *un*predictable future; back to improvisation.

As she slipped on her jeans and T-shirt and Emily folded and hung up the various pieces of her final ensemble, she committed to memory the numerous costumes she had enjoyed. She took off her makeup more slowly than usual, after taking one last look at the face of Leisl in the mirror.

So quickly. But she reminded herself that it had been good, and she hadn't blown it. Then there was Aaron . . . and the thought of him made it easier to smile.

"Ready for strike?" the now familiar voice greeted her as she stepped out of the dressing room.

"Oh, hi, Aaron. Strike—that's right, it's required, isn't it?"

"Yep," he said pleasantly, apparently glad for any excuse to be with Liz again. He was back in his jeans, flannel shirt, and glasses, his brown hair back in the shaggy, more natural style, his thumbs casually in his pockets.

Liz watched the set—the world in which she had lived for the past week—being dismantled before her eyes. She worked solemnly, in contrast to the girls who chatted casually about what they'd be doing later that evening and the young men who gleefully wielded hammers to separate the flats with as much noise as possible. As Liz reluctantly helped carry the flats out to the truck that waited to take them back to Krannert for storage, she felt a sense of loss

Chapter Twenty-three

mingled with fear, as though having found the perfect place to hide from some predator, she'd had her cover stripped away and now stood vulnerable and alone again.

And yet not alone, she reminded herself. There was Jesus. And there was Aaron. She had not yet spoken with one about the other, although she knew that she should. That morning, on the way to church, as she had been telling Sarah about Aaron, her friend had had but one point of interest: "Is he a Christian?" Liz had been a little embarrassed to tell her she didn't know, and a little annoyed with Sarah for asking such a practical, unromantic question. It had also annoyed her to have Sarah ask if she had prayed about the relationship. Liz had responded with something akin to "Well, duh!" but the fact that she hadn't yet taken the time to do so had something to do with her defensiveness. Perhaps she would pray about it after strike. But why did the thought make her uncomfortable?

She looked at the gentle soul in denim and flannel, helping cheerfully. God had made this dear person. Perhaps He had made him for her.

"Comin' through!" grunted a stagehand. Liz jumped out of the way of several students carrying a section of platform off the stage. She snapped out of her daydream and looked for someone to help, preferably Aaron.

The set having been dismantled and packed up, Liz returned to her dressing room for her belongings: her shoulder bag, her dancing slippers, a basket of flowers, and a red rose in a Coke bottle.

Aaron met her to help her carry her things back to her apartment, explaining with mock pouting that *he* had received no flowers on opening night, or any other night, for that matter. Liz responded by taking a daisy from her basket and sticking it through his buttonhole. Aaron seemed much more relaxed with Liz, and chatted freely as they walked.

"Funny how before the show you can be so scared to go on, then after it's over feel so bummed about it," he observed.

"You too? Well, it's nice to know I'm not the only one who feels that way. Only I wouldn't say I was exactly *scared* the first night."

"You weren't?"

"No. The word that comes to mind is . . . '*terrified!*'"

"Me too," Aaron laughed. "I'd get this horrible feeling like I was going to totally blow it." He hesitated, as if trying to decide whether or not to share the next bit of information.

"I have this dream sometimes where I'm in a show and I forget all my lines."

Liz stopped dead. "You're kidding! I have that dream all the time! Don't you *hate* it?"

"Yeah! I wake up in a cold swe—I mean, I wake up shaking."

"And *I* wake up in a *cold sweat*," said Liz. "You don't need to try to talk more refined around me."

"But," he protested with a smirk, "you're from Ladue!"

"That's *Lah-dee-doo*!" she corrected him, putting her nose in the air.

"Wow, you're good at that," he said, as though in awe. "But careful with your nose in the air. If it rains, you'll drown." They both laughed.

"I'm already missing the show," Liz confessed as she turned the key in her front door. "I'll be writing about it for a while in my journal—I've got some catching up to do."

"You keep a journal? So do I," said Aaron as he set the flowers on the kitchen counter.

"Really?" said Liz, delighted that they had one more thing in common. "Of course, if we're ever famous, they become memoirs," she explained.

"Well, you know what my favorite memoir of the show is?" he asked, turning to her.

"What?" she asked.

"Dancing with you," he said, looking into her eyes.

"We were good, weren't we?" she said smugly.

"Encore?" He extended his hand. She took it. And for the next few moments they hummed the familiar tune and went through the dance steps they'd learned so well. When the dance was over

Chapter Twenty-three

and the traditional moment of the kiss came, Aaron gently took her chin and lifted her face toward his.

The kiss was not on the forehead this time.

Chapter Twenty-four

"So where is it written, 'Thou shalt not date an unbeliever'?" Liz had tried to refrain from sarcasm up to that point, but she was becoming upset, and the turmoil within was making her defensive.

"'Do not be unequally yoked with unbelievers.' It's in Corinthians," Sarah said.

"Doesn't that have to do with marriage? I'm not marrying Aaron, I'm just dating him. Good grief!"

"But Liz, if you're dating, you could fall in love, and then what? You could be setting yourself up for a lot of pain."

"Or maybe by dating me, he could come to know the Lord."

"'Missionary dating?' Been there. It doesn't work. Dating is a distraction, not a witness. *Praying* for him would do a lot more good, believe me!" Sarah stated emphatically. Liz had never seen her this firm. "Besides, if you do fall in love with him, you might fool yourself with the same logic in regard to marriage."

"'Missionary marriage'? Give me some credit! What kind of idiot do you think I am?" As soon as she'd blurted out the words, Liz realized she had hit a nerve.

Counselor

Sarah was silent for a moment. "My mother did that," she said quietly.

Ouch!

"Oh Sarah, I'm sorry, I didn't mean . . ."

"Forget it," Sarah cut her off, determined not to get sidetracked from her mission. But then she seemed to reconsider and decide the story was worth telling.

"My dad's a great guy—he's the best. I guess Mom couldn't help falling in love with him. She was a brand new Christian, and she was convinced that God had sent him to her. She didn't know about the 'unequally yoked' passage, and nobody showed it to her. She thought by being his wife that she could bring him to the Lord eventually. She could see a lot of good in him. In fact, I think that if a person could get to heaven just by being a nice guy, my dad would be the first one they'd let in. He's always been faithful to my mom, never smoked, been drunk, read porn, or anything like that. He's always worked hard but wasn't a workaholic, has a great sense of humor—though sometimes he'll joke around when my mom's trying to talk about something serious; that makes her nuts! But he's always been a lot of fun. Like I said, the greatest."

"And the problem?"

"Liz, people *don't* get to heaven by being good. Dad didn't know Jesus, my mom did. She's stayed faithful to both of them, but her spiritual growth was something she could never share with Dad. Don't get me wrong, they've had a warm, loving relationship, and for the most part they're happy. But there's always that gap in the one area—and it's the most important area of Mom's life. She found out too late that it's really hard for someone like my dad to see himself as a sinner in need of a Savior. And, from the world's point of view, my dad's had a great life. He's had some crises, but nothing he couldn't handle by himself, or so he thought. And he's such a good man, it wasn't like he's some kind of blatant sinner. In a way that might have been better. He would have known he needed God." Sarah seemed sad. "And, all his children would have known, too."

"What do you mean?" Liz asked.

Chapter Twenty-four

"My older brother never came to the Lord, either. He saw my mom going to church and my dad staying home, and from all appearances Mom had more problems than Dad did. She was by nature moodier than he was, and there were times she'd seem so sad. Now I think I know what she was sad about. To love someone that much, and not even know if he's going to be in heaven..."

Liz could see what she meant, but then another thought occurred to her.

"But wait a minute, Sarah! If they hadn't gotten married, *you* wouldn't be here! I'd have a hard time being sorry *that* happened. I mean, all things do work out for good..."

"But not for the *best,* because we have free will to choose, and we don't always make the right choice. I have thought about that, though, and I think that if Mom had done it by the Book—if she had told Dad she wouldn't marry an unbeliever, he would've seen that the Lord was the most important person in her life, even over him. That would've been a more powerful witness than marrying him and hoping he'd change afterward. If she hadn't compromised, he might have been saved a long time ago. They might have been married anyway, and then their marriage could've had God at the center. Their marriage is good, but not everything it could have been."

"I had no idea," Liz murmured. She felt sick to her stomach as her defensiveness gave way to resignation. She liked Aaron, maybe even loved him, but it seemed clear what she had to do. "So, if I really care about Aaron..."

"You'll stay faithful to Jesus. Don't compromise!"

"I never thought of dating him as 'compromise.'"

"It's a risk, Liz. You could end up getting hurt badly—both of you."

"I know you're right. I hurt already. Your mom didn't know any better, but—"

"*You do.*"

"I guess I have no excuse, do I?"

Sarah gently but firmly summed it up: "If He isn't Lord of *all,* He isn't Lord *at* all." Seeing the tears and pain in Liz's eyes, she added reassuringly, "You never know, though, maybe your sticking to your guns will make Aaron come around."

"And maybe not," Liz added in a choked voice.

"Then you will have saved yourself a lot of heartache, *trust me*," said Sarah. "Better yet, trust God. His way is always best in the long run."

"I'm trying, it's just so . . . Oh Sarah, what am I going to say to Aaron?"

"The truth is a good idea."

"How'd you get so smart, Sarah?" she asked her for the second time.

"I told you, I've lived with the consequences."

"Oh yeah. Sarah?"

"Yeah?"

"What ever happened with your father?"

"Not much. He's still great, and sweet, and funny, and," she sighed, "content."

"Shoot."

"Yeah, tell me about it."

"And your mom?"

"She's happy. She has some really good friends from church, a prayer partner she's really close to, and," she smiled proudly, "she's got *me*."

"That must be a comfort to her."

"I think so." She smiled, as though remembering some secret joke. "We've had a lot of spiritual 'adventures' together. Prayers answered, situations turned around—neat stuff." Her smile faded. "But in that area, Dad's still an outsider."

Liz sighed. "You're right, that's not what I want in a relationship."

"May as well hold out for the best." Sarah gave her an encouraging smile.

"Yeah, I will. Just one thing . . ."

"What's that?"

Liz's eyes, now red and spilling over, met Sarah's. "Pray for me?"

Sarah hugged her. "I always have."

Chapter Twenty-five

Liz stood on the stage in full costume, her hair French braided, dancing shoes on her feet, and her heart in her throat. The familiar music was starting and she was drawing a blank. As she heard the notes, she remembered some lyrics, but most of them she remembered too late. The orchestra didn't stop for her, it just continued relentlessly as she tried frantically to find her place.

But all she could sing were bits and pieces of the song, between which the music carried on without her. She remembered the parts about being completely unprepared for life and how frightened and inexperienced she was, but there were great, embarrassing gaps as she fumbled for the words.

She began to realize that the stage crew was dismantling the scenery around her as she sang. What were the words now? Something about needing someone wise who could lead her in the right direction.

The crew carried off the last pieces of the set as the dance music played and Liz struggled to remember the steps. She looked to her partner for help, but was dismayed to find that, whether it was Steve or Aaron, he was not moving. As she stepped closer, she realized with horror that she was trying to dance with a mannequin, and the stage was now bare, leaving her alone in the spotlight.

Counselor

As total panic set in, she cried out a single syllable:
"J!"

Chapter Twenty-six

At a table for two at Armedo's Pizza, Aaron sat watching through the plate glass window as the endless stream of people rushed by on their way to classes, practices, jobs, meetings, or dates. While a few cars crawled slowly by, searching in vain for a parking spot, the majority of the crowd was on foot, and Aaron glanced at each one who hurried by. Suddenly his face brightened as he spotted an auburn-haired coed; she smiled at him and turned toward the door.

As she took her seat across from him, slightly breathless and flushed from her brisk walk, she seemed radiant; to Aaron, hers was the most beautiful face in the world.

"Sorry I'm late," Liz panted. "The phone rang just as I was on my way out the door, and—"

"Don't worry about it," Aaron reassured her. "You're here now, that's what's important."

Liz smiled back at him, luxuriating in the feeling of being wanted and appreciated that Aaron so often gave her. She felt like just basking in the warmth of that feeling for a while, and the thought crossed her mind that maybe she could talk to him about the matter at hand some other time.

Meanwhile, the country boy across the table was having thoughts of his own. The pizza shop was not exactly what one would call romantic, but there were few people there at this off-hour, and when Lone Star came on the radio singing "Amazed (Every Little Thing That You Do)," Aaron knew it was just the extra touch to make the moment complete. He felt supremely lucky to have found such a special lady. He felt unworthy, and yet the way it had all worked out, it had to have been fate—everything from Steve's well-timed illness to this moment with this song, the perfect song for lovers, especially when one of them was a guitar-playing country boy with a soft spot for romance.

He thought of when he first heard that song, a year or so before. It had been a hit on the country music charts then, and he was probably the only one in the theater department who had heard it. He had felt as though it were his own private song to dream by, and dream he had. He had imagined meeting that special someone someday, one to whom he could play his guitar and sing those heartfelt words. He had seen Liz and admired her from afar; he had dreamed of someone like her, but who would have guessed that a year later here he would be with Liz herself?

Now the song he had loved was a hit on the mainstream charts as well, and most students on campus were at least a little familiar with Lone Star. Now that his dream was in full bloom, it too was out in the open for all to see and envy. He wanted to freeze time and take it all in—the moment, the girl, the feeling, the song. Every word seemed so fitting—the way he felt about her, the way things were between them, and (though he was taking it slowly) the way he dreamed things would be someday.

Aaron saw in Liz's eyes a thoughtful, distant look, and he wondered whether she was having the same kinds of thoughts. Since the two of them were practically the only people in the place, the song couldn't be missed. The lyrics were clear. He reached across the table and took her hand.

If Aaron had known what Liz was actually thinking at that moment and what was giving her that faraway look, he would have been disappointed.

Chapter Twenty-six

She was hearing the same man singing the same song and looking across the table at her sentimental country boy. She was pondering what it was about that song that had drawn her to it when she had first heard it yet had seemed somehow "off." The melody that started out so familiar quickly took a turn in a different direction. What was it that was missing, and why was it that she felt tantalized every time she heard it? Suddenly she recognized a strain she had heard somewhere else, and the words came back to her, not a description of romantic love, but something deeper.

The singer continued his rhapsody about his woman, but then there it was again, that same elusive melody. It made Liz think of J, her comfort, her shelter.

It seemed that Liz's faith was affecting the way she heard things, even the similarities between a romantic country ballad and a love song that was even more intimate, the song of worship she had first heard that eventful night when she had given her heart back to her First Love.

So, while the radio played on about some songwriter's love affair and Aaron sang along silently, another song prevailed in Liz's heart. While the one song extolled all the little things the man liked about his lady, the things that pleased and satisfied him, the other was about total self-abandon, the commitment of one's whole life to an infinite God.

While being in love felt indescribably wonderful to Liz, still she knew that she could never let romance be the sole purpose of her life. She could see that this relationship, just like the unsatisfying song she was hearing, was lacking something, and that lack made it woefully off-center. The futility of continuing it was obvious, and her task was clear; she had to talk to Aaron about this, and it had to be now. No more putting off.

As her stomach closed in a tight knot and she realized how hopelessly weak her flesh was, she sent up a silent, desperate plea for help. She opened her mouth, not knowing if any sound would come out or not.

"Intervarsity's tonight," she said in a voice that tried to be casual but was not altogether steady. "Now that things have slowed down a bit, you wanna go?"

Counselor

As far as Aaron was concerned, this date had been very pleasant up until that point, although most of the "conversation" so far had come from Lone Star. Liz's sudden change of subject seemed to disturb him.

"Nah, I don't think so. You go ahead, though," he added with a cheerfulness that sounded somehow forced.

"That's what you said *last* week," Liz sighed. She swallowed hard. "Aaron, we've got to talk."

"Oh?" he replied, and the breeziness in his voice was still unconvincing.

"I've really enjoyed the times we've had together," she began, her voice shaking.

"So have I," he replied affectionately, his eyes meeting hers.

She looked at him for a moment, then looked away; if she was going to get through this, she could not be looking into those brown eyes.

"Aaron, I'm a Christian."

"I know, and that's OK with me," he replied agreeably.

"But . . . you're not. And that's *not* OK with me." Aaron looked hurt, but not altogether surprised. Liz felt a pang of guilt and started to pull back. *No!* she told herself. *You're not going to wimp out again!* Time and again she had attempted this conversation, and her tender heart and weakness had won out every time. *Not this time!* Liz continued in an unsteady voice, "My relationship with God is the most important thing in my life."

"More important than me." It was not a question.

Poor Aaron! she thought. *That must hurt.* Her heart went out to him. *But it's the Truth.* Liz sent out another prayer for strength and went on.

"Yes, more important than *anything*. Isn't that the definition of 'God'?"

"But do we have to have exactly the same beliefs to be . . . together? Do you think we have to have *everything* in common?"

"Well . . ." *Help me, Lord!*

"If you're looking for someone who is exactly like you in every way, you'll be looking for the rest of your life." He said it with such

Chapter Twenty-six

unexpected authority and appearance of wisdom that Liz was almost thrown off track. This was a side of Aaron she had not seen before.

"No, I don't think we have to have *everything* in common. But the important things, yes."

"I believe in God," he said defensively. "I try to live a good life. I don't get drunk or do any of the other stuff most students do. And you still think I'm a bad person?" He sounded wounded.

Boy, you're not making this any easier, are you?

"No, I think you're a very good person, about the nicest guy in the department. But,"—*How do I say this?*—"good isn't enough. And believing in God isn't enough. Most people believe in God, but when it comes to living their lives, they don't consult Him or obey Him, they just do their thing and hope that the 'Man upstairs' will take care of them. Like He's some kind of benevolent grandfather who's too senile to know what's going on. And then they wonder why their lives are messed up."

Aaron was silent for a moment. Liz, surprised at the way the words were now spilling out, felt a surge of confidence that she herself was not talking now, but that it was the Lord speaking through her.

"I've asked Jesus to be not just my Savior, but the *Lord* of my life. That means He's the center of my existence. He gave His life for me; the least I can do is give mine to Him. 'Lord' means He's in on every decision I make."

The words were now flowing so effortlessly that Liz found herself smiling just thinking about the One who was giving them to her.

"He's like this wonderful Counselor who's always with me, and always has the right answers, if I'll just do what He says. But better yet, He's not just *with* me, He's *in* me! Wouldn't you like to know God like that?"

OK, here was the moment. This was when Aaron was supposed to say, "What must I do to be saved?" Liz would lead him to the Lord, he'd be reborn, and the two of them would ride off into the sunset.

But apparently Aaron hadn't read that script. Instead, what he said was, "You're starting to sound like my mom." Liz couldn't tell

Counselor

if he said it with affection, amusement, or irritation—perhaps all of the above. "Believe me," he continued, "she's given me my share of preaching. I'm just not into the church thing. Some of her friends were so hypocritical and judgmental, it just really turned me off."

"But not all Christians are like that," Liz argued. "Do you think *I'm* like that?"

"It's starting to sound like it," he replied in a tone of bitterness that shocked her and cut her to the heart. "I thought we could have a good relationship based on what we do have in common. We both like theater—clean theater—we like to write, we enjoy our music, we're dreamers . . ."

"That's not enough," Liz interrupted, surprised to find her voice sounding more authoritative.

"Look, Liz, my dad's not a church-going Christian, and he and Mom do OK."

"Is that what you want—just 'OK'?"

"All right, they have a *good* relationship."

"I want more than good, Aaron, I want the *best*." She looked once more into his sad eyes, and again her voice wavered, but her resolve did not. "And that means Jesus has to be in the center. I'm sorry," she added decisively.

There seemed to be no more to say, yet Aaron looked so downcast that Liz couldn't bring herself to walk away. She felt short of breath, she wanted to cry, and though she knew she should not give him any encouragement at this point, she could not resist saying,

"I really do appreciate you, Aaron. You're kind, and thoughtful, and . . . sweet . . . You know, that rose you gave me—I never thanked you for that! It was the first time I ever got anything like that on opening night. I'll always remember the way it encouraged me, made me feel so special."

Aaron didn't answer but sat pensively processing what she was saying. If there was any chance that he could win her back, then he was willing to take credit for the token of esteem that had meant so much to her.

But the fact was, he hadn't given her the rose and had no idea who had.

Chapter Twenty-seven

The sanctuary was dark, except for the "exit" signs and the dim light that illuminated the cross behind the altar. As Liz's eyes adjusted to the darkness, she slowly and silently walked down the aisle to the altar. She knelt at the rail, staring at the cross that loomed ahead. It was both comforting and foreboding. She knew that Someone had loved her enough to give His life for her, and this reminder of the magnitude of that love gave her a welcome sense of security.

At the same time, she knew now in a very personal way that to love Him in return meant taking up her own cross and making certain sacrifices. She had just committed one act of surrender in obedience to Him, which turned out to be far more painful than she had imagined—for even with such love as God's, she still wanted human love as well. Her relationship with Aaron had been the first thing she had actually given up for Jesus, other than an hour's sleep, and it had been the first offering that had really meant something to her. All the other "sins" she had refrained from—the smoking, drinking, drugs, illicit sex—weren't in her nature to do anyway. Thus, she could hardly have considered her clean living a sacrifice. Such are the "sacrifices" of a child who decides to give up Brussels sprouts for Lent.

But breaking up with Aaron had been the hardest thing she had ever done, and she wondered, what else would she have to give up in order to serve Jesus? Would it be worth it? And what if she were to decide it wasn't? Where else would she go? If she couldn't trust God, whom *could* she trust?

With a heavy sigh, she covered her face with her hands and groaned, "Oh Lord, I'm so confused!" Startled at the way her voice broke the silence of that place, she continued her prayer in a whisper.

"I guess I was kinda hoping You would lay everything out for me now, show me what I'm supposed to do with my life. Sometimes I wish I could talk to You face to face, like we talked in my dreams. That was so wonderful . . . but then, I'd always wake up, and everything would be all murky again."

Then, for the first time since the dream that had changed her life, she remembered meeting J, and how difficult it had been to understand what he was saying at first. Yet, as she had learned to listen and had grown to love him, how quickly it had become easier, until she could understand every word effortlessly. Perhaps if she just continued to confide in the Lord, she could learn to hear His voice as clearly when she was awake.

"I loved doing *The Sound of Music*. But I think maybe my reasons for loving it were all wrong. I don't know if I'm supposed to be a full-time performer. I don't know if I could handle it—the ego thing. And, there are so few plays I think You'd approve of a hundred percent." She sighed, frustrated and too tired to sort it all out. With resignation she found herself saying, "I think maybe I majored in the wrong thing." A sense of déjà vu hit her. "Did You tell me that once?

"At the same time, I can't see just going back to St. Louis and working for Dad. Don't get me wrong, I love him—and thanks for giving me such great parents—but I don't think my heart would be in it. I want to do something I *know* You're calling me to do, and do it with a *passion*. I want to give You my *whole life* . . . I just don't know how!" With this, she laid her head in her arms and wept. She felt something of a release, but no clear answer came, just the

Chapter Twenty-seven

feeling that she wasn't alone. She listened hard but didn't hear God speak . . . or did she?

A voice, barely audible, was whispering not far from where she was kneeling. She straightened up, startled at the realization that someone else was there. She peered around her into the darkness. The whispering stopped, and a voice spoke clearly.

"Hi, Liz."

She spun around. "Who's that?"

"Just me." The voice was familiar but wasn't saying enough to positively identify. She could see the silhouette of a man in the back pew, where he had slipped in unnoticed. He stood and came down the aisle where his face became illuminated from the cross.

"Sean! What are you doing here?"

"Same thing as you, praying. Kinda hard to do at Krannert."

"No kidding. What're you praying about?"

"My future."

"I thought you had that all figured out."

"Oh," he said with an odd look on his face, "I still have some questions."

"Me too. Oh Sean, I'm so confused about everything! I want to serve Jesus, but I have no idea what He wants from me. Any guidance I get seems to always be just for a short time, and I can't see any farther ahead."

"'Your Word is a lamp unto my feet,'"* Sean quoted, as much to himself as to her.

"That's true, but for me the lamp doesn't seem very bright."

"Maybe it's supposed to be that way, so we'll trust Him a day at a time. If He gave it all to us at once, we'd be—well, *some* of us would be—off and running and trying to do it on our own, instead of letting Him do it. After all, it says 'a lamp unto my feet,' not 'a floodlight for the whole highway.'"

Liz thought about this for a moment. "Well, that's good to know. So it isn't just me. I guess not even human counselors give you the whole picture at once," she observed.

Sean paused, letting the idea sink in. "That's true. They take you through the steps one at a time." He glanced down and smiled, as if understanding a secret joke for the first time. Then, looking back up at Liz, he said encouragingly, "Don't worry if you can't see it all right away. Just work on what He's telling you now."

"Actually, I just did that. I believed He was telling me to break up with Aaron, and I did." She closed her eyes, trying to keep the tears from spilling out again. "It was *so hard!* I don't know what He wants me to do next, but if it's as painful as the last thing, I don't know if I'll survive."

Sean was silent a moment, then said, "Maybe the next thing won't be as hard. Just trust Him."

"That sounds real good when you say it—'one day at a time'—but with graduation coming, I'm going to have to make some decisions, and for me it looks like the path just came to a dead end."

"Believe me, I know the feeling," Sean confessed. "Tell you what, let's pray about it together. Jesus said that if two of us agree on something that's His will, He'll do it. I know it's His will for you to take the right next step. If we agree on it, maybe He'll show you tonight. I'll pray with you right now, if you want."

"Oh, would you?" Liz cried gratefully. "That'd be great!" As they bowed their heads, Sean took her hand and gave it a squeeze.

"Father," he began, "Liz really loves You and wants to serve You. Your Word says that if any of us lack wisdom, we can ask You, and You'll give it to us. Liz is asking for wisdom—and so am I—so we'll each know what You want us to do next. We're willing to trust You completely, and if it's one step at a time, that's OK, we just need to know the next step."

After a long silence, Liz looked up at the cross, as if hoping to see some kind of divine message written there. She could feel the warm hand covering hers, and found that it gave her both comfort and a sense of sadness.

"In a few short weeks, we'll all be going our separate ways," she said to Sean. "You, me, Sarah, everybody. Whenever I think about it, I get this knot in my stomach . . . sometimes I feel so alone," she sighed. "I know I shouldn't feel that way. I mean, I've got God, but . . ." Her voice trailed off.

Chapter Twenty-seven

"Adam had God, too," said Sean. "But the Lord still said, 'It's not good for man to be alone.'"** He watched her closely and took a deep breath before continuing.

"Maybe you shouldn't be trying to serve Him all by yourself," he went on. "Haven't you ever noticed that when Jesus sent people out, He sent them in pairs? It *isn't* right for man to be alone."

He paused, then added, "Or woman, either."

Liz tried not to resent the remark. But since she had experienced so much loneliness in the past four years, and as she now perceived herself once more to be alone in the world, this last implication was like a person saying to someone who was starving in the wilderness, "You know, you really should eat something."

"So when's He going to *send* me somebody?" she cried in frustration.

"What makes you think He *hasn't*?" cried Sean with equal frustration.

Liz looked at him, and for a moment it seemed as if a heavy fog were being lifted and she was seeing him for the very first time. Her friend—her brother in the Lord—was gazing at her with such earnestness, such care.

Such love.

In that instant her mind was flooded with memories of the past four years, like the pieces of a puzzle long scattered finally coming together before her eyes.

In that odd world of theater, where she had felt like a complete alien, there had always been one person who had been an encouragement to her. During the first awkward days of performing in class before virtual strangers, those times when one searches desperately for a friendly face, there had been one for her to focus on. When her nerves had started to take over, there had always been a pair of blue eyes that would wink at her and put her at ease. If she had given it any thought, she might have assumed that this was the way he treated everyone. His friendliness was certainly consistent. Later, upon learning that he was a Christian, she had attributed this kindness to Christ living in Him—and rightly so.

Counselor

But suddenly it struck her the way he had always seemed to be looking out for her. When she had finally landed a significant role in a play, it was one where he was the stage manager. Had he used his influence to persuade the director to cast her? He certainly hadn't congratulated *every* member of the cast who had clustered around the bulletin board that morning.

After the Friday performance, had he bent the rules a bit to let Sarah and Michael and other friends backstage to praise and encourage her? And the next day, had he spotted the woman with auburn curls in the crowded lobby and made himself available to direct George to his daughter's dressing room? Stage managers certainly weren't in the habit of opening the doors backstage to everyone's friends and family.

Or to a delivery boy from the florist, for that matter.

All these thoughts went careening through her mind, and quickly made their way from her head to her heart as she looked into her friend's eyes.

"You?" she murmured, in a voice that was barely audible.

"Why not?" he asked. The tone of voice was obviously meant to sound casual, but it betrayed the kind of anxiety that can only come from hope that has been building for years and now stands to be either fulfilled or shattered. Behind the precarious smile, he looked intently into her eyes.

Why not, indeed? she thought. As she realized just how much this friend meant to her, the answer seemed embarrassingly obvious.

"You've always been such a good friend to me," she said earnestly; she couldn't believe it had taken all this time for her to realize it. "I think I could easily see you as more than a friend." Seeing the unspeakable joy in his face, she asked, almost childlike, "And you'd be OK with that?"

"OK with it?" He exclaimed, hugging her. "I've been praying for it for years!" Again, she was stunned.

"You have?" she said, looking into his eyes again and seeing tears of joy. "I never—you never said anything, did anything . . ."

"Oh, I did plenty of praying."

Chapter Twenty-seven

"Yes, but usually a guy *does* certain things . . ."

"To advance his cause? Yeah, I know, but I wanted to make sure it was God doing it, not me."

"You just trusted Him to bring us together?" she gasped.

Instead of answering her, he got up. "I want to show you something," he said. He picked up a Bible from one of the pews and brought it back. He opened it in the middle and turned a few pages. "Here it is, the verse I've been standing on." He handed her the Bible. "Psalm 37:4."

Liz held it up to the dim light and read, "'Delight yourself in the Lord, and he will give you the desires of your heart.'*** So that's what you did, just delighted in Him. That's incredible."

"Well, He's in the business of doing incredible things."

Liz smiled and, being at a loss for words, simply laid her head on Sean's shoulder. It was something she had never thought of doing before that moment, yet it seemed as though she had waited to all her life. As he stroked her hair, she could hear him whispering over and over, "Thank You, Lord, thank You *so much*!" His arms were wrapped around her as if he were holding a delicate treasure, yet she sensed a strength in him that had long been there but had gone unnoticed or been taken for granted.

"I've never known someone who trusted God as much as you do," she said, still in awe of his faith. "But what about being 'unequally yoked'? I'm such a baby Christian, are you sure you want me?"

Sean laughed through his tears. "Liz, I've wanted you since day one."

As Liz let the statement sink in, she noticed he suddenly seemed uncomfortable.

"Let's go outside," he said.

The light breeze felt like the gentle breath of God as the pair walked together, hand in hand.

"So, how did you keep on trusting and believing?" Liz asked. "I mean, while I was being such an idiot and all."

Sean shot her a look of affectionate rebuke. "I'll deal with that 'idiot' remark later," he said. "Well, the Lord gave me encouraging signs along the way. Like when I started coming to Intervarsity and met Sarah. We got to be pretty good friends. I'll never forget the day she told me about her roommate, and I realized it was you and found out she had been praying for you, too."

"So it was a conspiracy!" Liz declared.

"Yep," Sean said with smug satisfaction. "Then the night I saw you walk into the IV meeting with Sarah, I knew God was at work. And when you prayed later to be saved—or to make sure you were—I knew that sometimes He works faster than we think He's going to."

"So you had to make sure I was a Christian first," Liz said, appreciating the wisdom of his priorities.

"Yeah. You kinda threw me for a loop, though, when you and Aaron got together. Up until then I'd never seen you in a relationship with a guy, and that had been encouraging, too. But then when you two paired up, I started to wonder if I'd just been indulging in wishful thinking all that time. But I also knew you were a Christian and Aaron wasn't, so I knew that wasn't right."

"Yet you never said anything to me."

"That's the sort of thing you needed to hear from God, or at least someone besides the one who would've liked to *replace* the heathen. Maybe I was just afraid you'd resent me if I interfered."

"I see what you mean. I might have."

"I tried to pray for whatever was right, even for Aaron's salvation. Man, was that hard! To be honest with you, I didn't know what to do, but I knew graduation was coming, and we'd likely go our separate ways. It seemed like time was running out, and I felt like I wanted to just go to you and risk telling you everything."

"Why didn't you?"

"I was going to, but I knew that I'd really need God's help—His strength, His words, His timing. So, I came to the church to get alone with Him for a while. You know, kinda throw myself on His mercy."

"Good plan."

"Then, when I realized you were here too, I wondered if the Lord was getting ready to finish the job."

Chapter Twenty-seven

"And He did. Isn't He amazing?"

"More than amazing," said Sean, grinning and shaking his head.

"And you—the way you trust Him is inspiring!"

"Hey, Liz, I'm surrounded by actors, who else am I gonna trust?"

"Good point."

"So . . . you wanna go somewhere?"

"Sure. Like where?"

"Well, how about the Chicago area? I hear there's this awesome church there that's starting up a drama ministry. They're gonna need someone to write their material. I mean, if you don't have any other plans for the next few years . . ."

* Psalm 119.105 NIV
** Genesis 2:18 NIV
*** Psalm 37:4 NIV

Chapter Twenty-eight

Liz awoke as if from a delicious dream. Immediately her mind was flooded with the wonderful realization that Sean was in love with her—and she was in love with him!

That wonderful person she had known all those years, first as a fellow theater student, then as a brother in Christ—the one she had been longing for had been right there all that time. Lying there and reminiscing about the past four years, she had to wonder: How could she not have known that he loved her?

He loved her! It seemed almost too good to be true. She remembered every detail of what had happened the night before, yet it seemed like a dream. She felt a sudden pang of fear. What if it *had* been a dream? One of her vivid, emotional, heart-rending dreams! She couldn't bear the thought, yet there was no tangible evidence that the encounter she remembered had really taken place.

Oh God, tell me that wasn't a dream! she prayed. She was ninety-nine percent certain that it hadn't been, yet the one percent doubt was enough to make her joy incomplete. It nagged at her like the buzzing of an obstinate fly.

As if in answer to her prayer, the phone rang. She fumbled for the receiver and said hoarsely, "Hello?"

"Liz, this is Sean—did I wake you?"

Sean had called before, but only in regard to Intervarsity or theater. But although a call from him was rare, still it did not give her the complete reassurance she needed.

"Are you OK, Liz?" he asked hesitantly.

"Um, yeah, I'm fine," she responded, not sounding at all fine.

Sean paused. "You aren't having second thoughts about us, are you?" he asked anxiously.

Us. Such a small word, so much meaning.

"Second thoughts?" She laughed with sheer relief. "No! Not in the least!"

Epilogue

*I*f you're expecting me to tell you "They lived happily ever after," think again. That would only mean "nothing interesting or exciting happened after that." And, as J once told Liz, her life would *never* be boring. She had embarked on the adventure of a lifetime, and the journey had just begun.

TO BE CONTINUED.

To order additional copies of

Counselor

Have your credit card ready and call:

1-877-421-READ (7323)

or please visit our web site at
www.pleasantword.com

Also available at:
www.amazon.com
www.barnesandnoble.com

Printed in the United States
1008800005B